DJ TAYLOR

POPPYLAND

SALT
MODERN
STORIES

SALT

CROMER

PUBLISHED BY SALT PUBLISHING 2025

2 4 6 8 10 9 7 5 3 1

First published in Great Britain in 2025 by
Salt Publishing Ltd
12 Norwich Road, Cromer, Norfolk NR27 0AX United Kingdom

GPSR representative
Matt Parsons matt.parsons@upi2mbooks.hr
UPI-2M PLUS d.o.o., Medulićeva 20, 10000 Zagreb, Croatia

www.saltpublishing.com

Salt Publishing Limited Reg. No. 5293401
A CIP catalogue record for this book is available from the British Library

ISBN 978 1 78463 346 2 (Paperback edition)
ISBN 978 1 78463 347 9 (Electronic edition)

Typeset in Granjon by Salt Publishing

Printed and bound in Great Britain by Clays Ltd, Elcograf S.p.A

D.J. TAYLOR has written thirteen novels, including *Trespass* (1998) and *Derby Day* (2011), both of which were longlisted for the Man Booker Prize, and three volumes of short stories, most recently *Stewkey Blues* which won the Fiction Award in the 2022 East Anglian Book Awards. His non-fiction includes *Orwell: The Life*, which won the 2003 Whitbread Prize for Biography, and its successor, *Orwell: The New Life* (2023). He lives in Norwich with his wife, the novelist Rachel Hore.

Their beauty has thickened.
Something is pushing them
To the side of their own lives.

PHILIP LARKIN, 'Afternoons'

*Dave, Rodney, Stevie, Spike, Eddie, Horace, Richard,
Shaun and all the other Norwich boys*

Contents

Poppyland

THEY CAME DOWN the winding asphalt path from the cliff-top in their usual holiday phalanx: Danny in front, guiding the buggy; Marigold a step or two behind him; Mr and Mrs Callingham vigilant on the flanks. At the bottom of the slope there were a couple of herring gulls tearing open an abandoned fish-and-chip packet, but the sight of Mrs Callingham in her saffron summer frock was too much for them and they flapped noisily away. *Bird*, Archie chirruped from the buggy – it was one of the five words he knew, along with 'bean,' 'bath-time,' 'banana,' and 'Ummagumma,' his pet monkey – *bird, bird, bird, bird*, and Danny leant forward and patted him fondly on the head. The herring gulls were gone now, heading out over the pier into the duck-egg-blue sky, bound for the Hook of Holland for all anyone knew. *Bird* Archie said one last time and then went silent. Down at the foot of the cliffs it was unexpectedly cold and the shadow cast by the hand-rails fell dramatically across the pavement. Danny, bringing the buggy to a halt, glanced surreptitiously at the figures assembled around it: Marigold, dutifully attentive to whatever her mother was saying; Mrs Callingham, blithe, stork-like and terrifying; Mr Callingham a more solid presence, but, Danny knew, liable to cause trouble if not closely watched.

'Well, this is all very picturesque,' Mrs Callingham said, propping one of her huge bony knees upon the bottom-most rail. Unlike many of Mrs Callingham's opinions this one, Danny acknowledged, had something to be said for it. The steps running up to the pier entrance had panels sunk into them which recorded the exploits of the Cromer Lifeboat. On the wall beyond hung posters of Freddie Starr, the Nolan Sisters and other veteran acts who were appearing in Summer Season. It was about ten o'clock in the morning, still early for the holiday crowds, and not bad for mid-July. 'I used to come here as a boy,' he began to explain, feeling unexpectedly proprietorial about the row of beach huts and the criss-cross of anglers' lines, but Mrs Callingham was not in the mood for childhood reminiscences. 'I had a long conversation with Fenny,' she said, addressing herself to Marigold, 'and she had some good news and some bad news. The bad news is that Angelica has failed her driving test, but the good news is that Mark's psoriasis is improving.' Defying the urge to add 'as if anyone cared,' Danny looked to see how his father-in-law was taking this update on his wife's sister's family, but Mr Callingham, who had not yet found a newsagent able to sell him a copy of *The Times,* was still sunk in gloom.

'That's a shame about Angelica,' Marigold said absently. She was still exhausted from the previous afternoon's three-hour drive and the sleepless night with Archie. Another day or so and she would be able to give these

Clan Callingham gossip-fests all the punctilious gusto they deserved. The Callinghams, who answered to 'Billa' and 'Geoffrey', were reaching the end of their stratospherically distinguished careers. Billa taught medieval history at one of the smaller Cambridge colleges and had written a 'seminal' book about Angevin Shropshire, while Geoffrey did something so mercurially abstruse at the Foreign and Commonwealth Office that Danny had never actually managed to work out what it was. Four years on, he was still amazed that they had allowed him to marry their daughter. 'Of course,' Mrs Callingham was saying, with a certain amount of bitterness and in a blizzard of phantom italics, 'it'll be a *great advantage* when she does pass her test because I dare say she'll be able to *drive down* and visit you.' And Danny knew that they were back to the conversation that had enlivened, or strictly speaking undermined yesterday's trip along the A12. 'Oh, Mum,' Marigold said, 'it's only something we're talking about. Something to discuss.' There were times when he thought the Callinghams were a well-meaning but censorious and interfering old couple and other times when he thought the four of them were engaged in a no-holds-barred power-struggle that made the Wars of the Roses – about which Mrs Callingham had written illuminatingly – look tame by comparison. Desperate for a diversionary tactic, he tapped Archie on the shoulder with sufficient heft to make him swivel slightly in his seat and then said with apparent surprise: ' You know, I think Arch has another tooth coming through.' This did the trick. Mrs Callingham, whose attitude to children was that of Grace Darling towards water-boatmen, went down on one knee and grabbed at Archie's face between her coal-heaver's fingers. 'Poor ickle babbity,' she pronounced, with no self-consciousness whatever. 'Is oo's toofy-pegs hurting um?' *Naughty* toofy-pegs.' Amid the clamour of the gulls and the roar of the water crashing against the sea-defences, tiny, insignificant figures dwarfed by the wide horizon, they made their way down to the beach.

After that things improved slightly. Mr Callingham found a kiosk on the front that sold newspapers and settled down to read about the war in Iraq. Mrs Callingham ate an ice-cream in a mincing, girlish way and gave exaggerated little shrieks of disquiet as fragments of the chocolate flake tumbled down the front of her dress. Marigold unfurled a towel on the sand, lay down on it and fell instantly asleep. Archie, unleashed from his buggy, tottered a few steps here and there, collapsed in a tumble of misplaced limbs, tried to eat a worm-cast and said a sixth word, which might have been 'Diogenes.' Still, though, danger lurked in all this seemly repose. Mrs Callingham relayed some more urgent family news about someone called Francesca, who might or might not have been sent to Indonesia by whoever it was that employed her, before offering some startlingly unoriginal remarks about the Government's education policy. Mr Callingham, benign and rubicund in open-toed sandals and rolled-up flannel trousers, got as far as the Arts pages of *The Times* and then gave an ominous snuf-fle. 'There's a man here *really* doesn't like your book,' he declared.

This kind of thing had happened before. With infinite weariness – not because he feared the reviewer's strictures, but because he feared the conversation that would follow his reading of them – Danny lent forward, discovered that for some reason Mr Callingham was not prepared to relax his grip on the paper, but eventually gathered from glancing over his shoulder that Daniel Foxley's third novel was an undistinguished performance that harboured few of the qualities intermittently on display in its predecessors. 'Friend of yours, is he, this I. B. Littlejohn?' Mr Callingham wondered in a half-way jovial tone, and Danny smiled back. 'We were at college together,' he riposted, and then, for good measure, 'He taught me all I know.' Mrs Callingham was having one of her vague moments, when the warp and weft of the world escaped her usually circumspect eye, but in the end Mr Callingham managed to explain to her what had happened, and she, too, was allowed a grudging glance at *The Times*. 'You really are *not* to worry about this,' she instructed him. Mrs Callingham's attitude to Danny oscillated wildly. Early on in their relationship she had told Marigold, not wholly approvingly, that he was 'rather a high-flier.' Just lately she had been heard to say that these provincial universities were making great strides. 'When we get home,' she said fiercely, as if someone were purposely delaying her journey there, 'I'll make us all lunch. That is, if one can find a serviceable saucepan.' After that they sat there in silence under the wide sky, while children shrieked and cantered around them, until such time as Marigold woke up and they could collect their things, find the car and drive off through the Norfolk back-lanes, the head-high clumps of cow parsley and the shimmering fields of poppies.

◊

The holiday let was three miles out of Cromer at the end of a lane of beech trees: elegant, spacious, cool even in summer. Mrs Callingham's way of finding fault with it was to go fossicking around the kitchen drawers lamenting the absence of items no ordinary person could ever want: an egg-whisk and a cake-knife were high on this list of desiderata. Danny knew already that the visitor's book, which lay on the hall table next to a Bakelite telephone and a gazetteer called *What to do on the Norfolk Coast,* would not be safe from her. For lunch Mrs Callingham cooked an Irish Stew, heavy on the onions and with additional clumps of pearl barley lurking in its lower depths. In the intervals of eating it, and trying to interest Archie in a warmed-up jar of savoury rice, and watching the Calling-hams absently-mindedly clash water-glasses together and knock over salt-cellars, Danny found himself wondering, as he quite often did, what kind of people they were. When first ushered into their presence in the big, cacophonous house at Harrow-on-the-Hill, he had assumed that they were old-fashioned, high-minded liberals of the sort he had read about in books about the Bloomsbury Group, only to discover that Mr Callingham, at least, quite liked talking about money and reading the *How to Spend It* section of the *Financial Times.* 'My mother is a very straightforward person,' Marigold used to maintain, which was true in one way and so transparently false in another as to make you wonder whether her occasional bouts of plain-speaking weren't an elaborate smokescreen thrown up to disguise the extraordinarily complex mixture of will-power, abstraction and downright craziness by which Mrs Callingham lived her life. In the end he decided that the Callinghams,

Billa and Geoff, Professor Wilhelmina Callingham PhD., F.R.H.S, and Geoffrey Callingham OBE, were simply two wonderfully eccentric and self-propelled people whom chance had thrown together and sent spinning forward while the rest of humanity cowered in their wake, that they would offer marvellous parts for someone to play in a film but were rather less appetising when you had to live cheek-by-jowl with them for weeks at a stretch.

'You would think that this place would run to a *ladle*,' Mrs Callingham complained, dumping another pile of onions on Danny's plate. After lunch, knowing what he was letting himself in for but determined to do his best, he volunteered for the washing-up and dealt politely with the imperfectly-rinsed cutlery while Mrs Callingham talked about some friends of hers who had moved to Lincolnshire and really lost touch and how very susceptible certain parts of the South-west were to flooding – further oblique references, as he well knew, to the conversation of the previous day. Archie, returned to his buggy, had fallen asleep. Mr Callingham, now barefoot and be-shorted, sat watching cricket on the TV. Leaving Billa with a book called *Planning for Dystopia*, he went into their bedroom and found Marigold stretched out on the bed with her arms and legs extended in the shape of a Maltese Cross.

'How was the washing-up?'

'It was a blast. I put all the forks in the fork compartment and all the knives in the knife compartment and then your mother came and mixed them up again. After that she started telling me about some friends of hers who moved out of London and they ended up feeling so isolated that the husband went mad and tried to shoot himself. Oh, and how wonderful she thinks Arch's day-nursery is and how nice all the girls who work there are.'

'You can hardly blame her for that. Not after Etta and Sophie. We're the only ones left in town.'

It would have been wrong, Danny knew, to tell Marigold that there was a reason why one of her sisters lived in Newcastle and the other in North Wales, so he smiled in what he thought was a sympathetic way.

'Did you ring work?'

'No I didn't.' Marigold did the marketing for a high-end stationery concern that sold monogrammed notepaper and envelopes in a variety of aquarelle washes. 'I left instructions for the press release to be sent out on Thursday, and if anybody rings up Rebecca will just have to deal with it herself.' She chewed at her lower lip in a way he always found irresistible. 'How do you think Dad is?'

There was no way of honestly answering most of the questions Marigold asked about her parents. How did he think Geoffrey was? Slightly more pompous and slightly less affable than usual? Far too fat? It was difficult to tell.

'Seemed on good form. He was wearing a pair of shorts last time I looked. Really getting into the spirit of the afternoon.'

This kind of bantering never worked with Marigold. She was a serious girl, and never more so than when the talk turned to members of her family and how they were feeling about things.

'Mum says he's a bit worried. Apparently someone's been complaining about a treaty he helped draft for the Turks and Caicos Islands back in the 1980s. Something to do with not apportioning mineral rights.'

Danny had a sudden vision of vengeful islanders denied their cobalt and lithium dancing upon the Caribbean strand as they burned Geoffrey in effigy. But it did not do to dwell on these things. What he really wanted, he thought, was to take Archie for a walk through the poppy fields, far away from Geoffrey in his horrible shorts and the look of savage exaltation on Billa's face as she dropped the cutlery into the wrong compartment.

'If we did decide to go and live there,' Marigold said, suddenly brisk and purposeful, face aglow under her thatch of blonde curls, 'What am I supposed to do?'

'Well you wouldn't have to sit there listening to Rebecca drone on about the Duchess of York. And you know you've always said you wanted to set up on your own.' Marigold bent her head, which was a start, but he knew that this was not what the conversation was really about. 'Look,' he said, knowing that he was overplaying his hand, 'you can't spend your whole life conciliating your mother.'

'But that's what you have to do, isn't it?' Marigold said, not exactly miserably but with considerably more emphasis than she put into most statements about human behaviour. 'You conciliate people and you put up with them, because of what you owe them.' Beyond the door he could hear Archie emit one of those little yells that meant he was tired of listening to Billa asking him if he had enjoyed his ickle sleepie or having her wave brightly-coloured lengths of silk above his head. 'Do you know Etta says she rings them three times a week? And she's offered to pay all Ceridwen's nursery fees.'

There was no gainsaying this, Danny thought. Maternal affection was sacrosanct. All the same, it made you want to enumerate some of the things that putting up with people entailed. In his own particular case it meant having them come on holiday with you and severely limiting your room for manoeuvre while they were there. It meant them giving your children ridiculous nicknames – Billa had started off trying to call Archie 'Archers' before settling on 'Arch-Warch' – while not registering the pained look on your face. It meant being subjected to a constant barrage of information about distant relatives you might have met at your wedding but would never see again. It also involved – and this, too, had to be allowed – being thoroughly exasperated by people who meant well while remaining heroically unaware of the annoyance they were causing.

'We ought to go and see how Archie is,' Marigold said, and then, just to make sure that he knew she was still in a bad mood, 'Gosh I'm tired.'

They went into the main room to find Archie staring grimly at a pile of Lego bricks, Geoffrey still watching the cricket and Mrs Callingham collapsed into a cane chair with the peculiarly glazed and stricken expression that he remembered from previous holidays. Billa's headaches were not to be trifled with. Genuinely sympathetic, for once, Danny brewed tea, fetched glasses of water and hunted out Ibuprofen capsules from the vast pharmacopeia Marigold had brought with them. Separating out the emotions that these acts bred up in him, he realised that he was pleased with himself for the show of willing, cross with himself for permitting an unwonted level of self-congratulation, contemptuous of anyone who succumbed to anything so trivial as a headache and disgusted with himself for his lack of fellow-feeling, while darkly aware that all this complexity was part and parcel of what life with the Callinghams was like, as soul-sapping and ineradicable as all the plastic micro-globules strewing the ocean floor. *Bird-bird-bird-bird-bird* Archie carolled, who had presumably glimpsed one outside the window, 'Has 'oo seen an ickle birdie, den?' Mrs Callingham began, but then gave up the struggle and held her head in her hands. Outside the sunshine fell over the bright green grass.

◊

Slowly the long days passed. Sometimes they headed north along the coast. Other times they went inland in search of supermarkets or places where Mr Callingham could buy the *New Statesman*. They went to Holkham, looked around the park and listened to Mrs Callingham criticise some of the portrait attributions. They attended art exhibitions in village halls set back from the coast road, examined the pictures of crab-boats in Blakeney harbour or terns taking flight off Stewkey marshes and drank cups of pale tea from urns drawn up on rickety trestle tables. They went to the Smoke House at Cley and stocked up on pickled herrings and jars of anchovies. Occasionally the old world they had left behind intruded. It turned out that the girl who had been supposed to send out the press releases had gone home sick before she had had time to do it, and Marigold had to spend an hour on the phone repairing the damage. A newspaper rang up and asked Danny for a comment piece about some pictures of Madonna at the gym ('Interesting things you get to write about,' Mr Callingham observed when it was shown to him the following morning.) There was another, better review of Danny's novel in the *Daily Telegraph* ('Isn't he a friend of yours too?' Mr Callingham wondered.) Mr Callingham had cheered up a bit and seemed to have forgotten about the Turks and Caicos mineral rights.

Formula milk heated up in a plastic bowl. Baby rice. Calpol. Teething rusks. Tumbled Lego bricks. 'Gosh I'm tired.' Sometimes the routines they had spent so long devising fell away and new patterns emerged. Out walking the back-lanes or striding inland through the waist-high grass, the old phalanx was abandoned and they marched in single file, Mrs Callingham prospecting along the path and talking to Marigold over her shoulder. Wondering whether he was supposed to hear the gusts of conversation which rattled back and forth, some of which were surprisingly intimate and several of which concerned himself, Danny decided that it had simply not occurred to Mrs Callingham that he might be within earshot. She was famous in Cambridge circles for once having given her opinion of one student to a second student without realising that the first one was seated next to her on the sofa. Still, it was nice to know that the mother of the woman you were married to reckoned you *fundamentally good-hearted* if *prone to hasty decision-making.* But how would he have fared on that college sofa? Danny trembled to think.

Ironically, in the light of what came after, the trip to Ranworth, half-way through the second week, was Mrs Callingham's idea. It was she who turned out to have mugged up on the Broads, and she who had identified the great tall church with its view out over the Norfolk flats as worth an hour or two of their time. They took a packed lunch, set off early along the coast road through the tourist traffic and the hopper buses and then cut inland through the reed-beds. *Banana* Archie sang. *Banana, banana.* There had been another urgent colloquy about their relocation the previous evening. In its bruising aftermath Danny couldn't quite tell if he was wearing the opposition down or being worn down himself. One good omen, he supposed, was that Marigold, telephoned at 8 p.m. by the Duchess of York-toadying Rebecca, had actually put the receiver down on her. Fetched up at the church, with its soaring flint tower and the mass of dark water stretching away into the middle distance, he was surprised at how small everyone seemed. Mrs Callingham, unloading cagoules from the back of the car, looked a frail and insubstantial figure, there on sufferance, ripe to be swept away. Archie, asleep in his buggy as the dragonflies swarmed over his head, was a tiny embellishment on the edge of the frame. Downcast by this hint of his own insignificance, Danny pressed on into the church's interior, which was cool and dim and there was a smell of furniture polish. He liked churches and found their atmosphere consoling. Mrs Callingham, too, was manifestly enjoying herself. She found a pile of prayer-kneelers that had slipped out of trim and zealously restored them to order, and then sped down the aisle casting indulgent glances at the carved pew-ends. A bit later her eye fell on the doorway that allowed access to the tower.

'Shall we *ascend*?' she wondered in the faultless parody of a Victorian noblewoman that she sometimes affected on special occasions.

'Well, I'm keeping my feet on the ground,' Mr

Callingham volunteered, tapping the rim of the buggy with a fat hand. 'Someone's got to look after His Lordship here.'

'There's a hundred steps, Mum,' Marigold said, who had also read the guidebook. 'And then a couple of ladders before you get to the roof. Are you sure you wouldn't be better off staying here?'

'It will be an *adventure*,' Mrs Callingham said, reprising the girlish glee with which she had eaten the ice-cream cone.

And so they set off, Danny leading the way, Mrs Callingham following, Marigold bringing up the rear. The church was silent except for the slither of their footsteps and, from below, a faint growling noise which Danny supposed was Mr Callingham trying to entertain his grandson. The staircase was circular and rose sharply. Danny put on speed and came out on a wooden platform that contained the church bells and the first of the two ladders, stopped for a second or two to catch his breath and then pressed on to the roof. There was no sound coming from below so he went forward to the parapet, laid his arms lengthways on the stone and gazed out over the broad, where boats were tacking back and forth in the breeze and what looked like a kayak race was in progress in the corner. On the far shore the woods sloped down to the water's edge and it needed only a couple of greybeards stretched out under a tree and a glimpse of a ruined temple to make you think you were in a painting by Claude Lorrain.

'Danny, you'd better come down,' Marigold said anxiously as she came out onto the roof to join him.

'Why's that?'

'It's Mum. She's stopped three quarters of the way up. She says she can't go on anymore.'

'Well, tell her to go back down.' He was still cross about the vision of Claude Lorrain being prised from his grasp.

'It's not as simple as that. She says she's stuck. She's always had this thing about heights. You know, freezes up and can't move.'

'How did you get past her then?' He was quite interested in this as a scientific problem. 'I mean, if she's stuck fast?'

They hurried back down the ladder, bounded over the belfry platform and rapidly negotiated the steps. At head level there was ancient graffiti carved into the brickwork that said GWD and EY had been here in 1894, and he wondered what sort of time they'd had. Mrs Callingham had come to rest next to a tiny niche in the wall, one arm angled slightly forward from her body and the other angled slightly back, as if she were frozen in the act of running, and he stopped abruptly and sized her up.

'What's the matter, Billa?'

'It's very stupid of me,' Mrs Callingham said almost skittishly, 'but I just can't move.'

'Well, you can't stay here. Are you able to turn round?'

'No, I'm not. It would be all right if I wasn't in this *enclosed space*,' Mrs Callingham explained, as if it had been very stupid of whoever had designed the tower not to have realised that she might want to climb up it several hundred years later.

'Well, you'll just have to come down backwards.' He managed to squeeze past, coax Mrs Callingham onto the steps, grasp one of her hands and tug her into reverse. 'Be careful,' Marigold cried from three steps above. 'Really, I'm quite all right,' Mrs Callingham said. The process of extracting her took half an hour. At the bottom of the stairs they found several people waiting to go up. 'I'm very sorry to have delayed you all,' Mrs Callingham said brightly, before unexpectedly bursting into tears.

◊

All that last morning at the house, as Mr Callingham harumphed about and Marigold turned up items of baby equipment in odd places, he found himself wondering what Mrs Callingham would write in the visitor's book. Would she complain about the paucity of casserole dishes? The noise the cistern in the upstairs loo made when you flushed it? The way the overgrown honeysuckle clanged against the downstairs window when the breeze got up? These were all plausible candidates. In the end, though, picking up the book when her gaze was elsewhere, he discovered she had written only that the Callingham/Foxley party had enjoyed a very pleasant stay in a well-appointed holiday home and might easily return one day. If this was a small victory, then a larger one had manifested itself on the previous evening when Mrs Callingham had conceded that bringing up a young family in London didn't suit everyone and that Marigold was looking rather tired these days.

Still, though, you needed to be sure. He knew from bitter experience that where the Callinghams were concerned, nothing could ever be taken for granted. They had almost finished loading up the car – Billa and Geoffrey in the back on either side of the baby seat, Archie with

Ummagumma dangling from the fingers of one hand, the tea-towels and recipe books they had bought in stately homes along the way parcelled up in the glove-compartment – when Mr Callingham, who had an OS map of East Anglia open on his knee, said: 'If I were you I'd head for Lowestoft and take the A12.'

'Actually,' Danny said, keen to press home his advantage, 'I thought the A11 would be a better bet.'

A bit later they set off along the beech avenue, where glimmers of yellow light broke through the tree canopy and the squirrels sat motionless in the branches as if they had never seen a car before and wondered what horrors it might portend, and then off through the wheat-fields, where the poppies, crimson and consoling, shimmered at their side.

Moving On

Kᴇᴠ ᴀɴᴅ Cʜʀɪꜱꜱɪᴇ get the keys to 18 Hodgson Road, Norwich in January 1983. Kev is nineteen and Chrissie a year younger, but there is a marriage certificate behind the clock on the mantelpiece in the front room where Chrissie also keeps the rent book and the passport that accompanied her on a day-trip to Boulogne four years back, and Kev's Aunty Sheila, who has influence in these matters, has put in a word at the City Council Housing Department. Aunty Sheila has been renting council houses all over the west side of Norwich for thirty years and knows what to do. She is a big, shapeless woman – twice the size of Kev's diminutive mum – who runs a fruit and veg stall on Norwich market. Kev says the house is a good place to start off – handy for Bunnett Square and its double row of shops and at the end of a bus-route that will take Kev to his job, which is at the Jarrold print works in town. Among other items, Jarrold's manufactures picture-postcards of Norfolk scenes: Yarmouth seafront; Holkham beach; Thetford Forest. Sometimes Kev brings a pile of them home in his knapsack and they use them for shopping-lists. Looking out into the back garden on winter afternoons – it is mostly concrete terrace, but there is a patch of grass and a plastic swing that the last tenants left behind – Chrissie thinks the house will do. She is a pale, serious girl with two 'O' levels (English Literature, Home Economics) and a tendency to asthma. Kev has no qualifications, unless you count the St John's Ambulance Brigade certificate that he acquired in the Boy Scouts.

Somehow Kev and Chrissie never settle at No. 18. The house smells of damp, there are rats in the walls and the Brannigans, who live next door, have a habit of throwing parties that go on all weekend, with the children scampering around in the backyard until the small hours. One of these days, Kev says, he will have words with Mr Brannigan. Somehow he never does. Still, they like going to the Romany Rye on the far side of the square, or the Volunteer half a mile away on Earlham Road, which has the additional advantage of running Friday-night sweepstakes. At one of these Kev wins £40 of prime butcher's meat and they spend the next fortnight gorging on lamb steaks, back bacon and some weird, gamey stuff which Kev says is venison. It is about this time that Kev comes home from work with that serious expression she remembers from the days when he used to sit arguing with his parents and says there is this place he has heard about in Fairfax Road and would she like to take a look? It is private rental, Kev says, but cheap and there is a nice garden and a primary school not far away, which will come in handy when the baby – Chrissie is three months pregnant – arrives. Fairfax Road is on the other side of the estate towards Eaton Park and Northfields, but Chrissie knows people there and doesn't mind. On the evening they walk across to inspect the premises, the Brannigans are having one of their parties and somebody has tipped a bin over in the street. Good riddance to bad rubbish, Kev says.

Chrissie adores the flat, which is on the ground floor and takes the light. There are two bedrooms and she earmarks the second as a nursery, stencils outlines of fish on the walls and makes a mobile out of old coat-hangers and soft toys to dangle over the cot. The baby is born in July – it is 1986 now, and Norwich are back in the First Division – and Kev's mum and dad come round to pay their respects. Kev and his parents have never got on, not ever, Kev says, but a baby is a big thing and differences have to be put aside. Long years later Chrissie will come upon a photo, taken by a neighbour, of the four of them sitting in the garden on under-sized chairs brought out from the tiny kitchenette staring at the baby – Emma-Jane she is called – as she lies on a blanket, Kev's parents placid and benign. Already Kev has that restless, intent look clouding his features. Norwich is a small place, he says: it wears you down. But Chrissie disagrees. To her Norwich is a big, teeming city. There are parts of it – Spixworth, Sprowston, Heartsease – where she has never been. What lies beyond is unimaginably remote. This attitude, she know, is quite common. Her Aunty Steph, who lives in Shotesham, eight miles away, has only left Norfolk three times in her life.

The Fairfax Road flat lasts two years. On bright summer forenoons Chrissie takes Emma-Jane out to Eaton Park to look at the giant carp basking in their artificial lake or have tea in the bandstand café. There is a story that someone once put a pike in the carp pond which caused such havoc that it had to be retrieved by a professional angler. Other times they go round to see Chrissie's mum, who lives near the row of shops on Colman Road and gives Chrissie packets of ice-cream out of her deep-freeze. Kev has a new job now as security guard at the Norwich Union office in Surrey Street in the city centre. There are times when he has to work nights, prowling up and down the empty corridors with a flash-light, but Kev says he doesn't mind. Then one day in the summer of 1988 they get a letter to say that their landlord has bought the upstairs flat and intends to redevelop the property. It is all because of the Government selling off council houses, Kev says, and there is nothing you can do. Kev approves of Mrs Thatcher, but he is cross about the flat.

Still, Norwich is a big city. There are always places to live. If it comes to it, Kev says – he is in his mid-twenties now, and his face, pale from the night-shifts, is starting to fill out – they can go and stay with his parents for a while, save money and take their time, but Chrissie knows this will never work. In any case, there is another baby on the way. In the end, through Aunty Sheila, Kev hears about a council flat on the Mile Cross estate, just off the Inner Ring Road Kev says, who goes over to inspect it one autumn afternoon, but with a cheap rent on account of some of the fixtures needing renewing. Chrissie has her doubts about the flat – Mile Cross is a rough area, where the police are supposed to go in twos – but there is no stopping Kev when he has an idea in his head and so the tenancy agreement is signed, Kev borrows a van from a mate, and with the aid of Chrissie's dad they spend a winter day just before Christmas moving in. Chrissie's dad, sipping from a beer can Kev has handed him now the job is done, says he hopes it all works out, and Chrissie, feeling the baby move within her, hopes so too. A jet blows up in the sky over Scotland and hundreds of people are killed, and Kev says you wouldn't get him on an aeroplane if you paid him.

Mile Cross is not a success. The flat is on the third floor and the slippery concrete steps are full of horrors: used condoms and dog mess aren't the half of it. There is a patch of waste ground outside where the kids come and light fires in the night and a mad old lady from one of the downstairs flats who runs out screaming in her dress-ing-gown, or sometimes not even that, until a neighbour comes along to fetch her in. One of these days, Kev says, he will give the lairy kids a piece of his mind. Somehow he never does. Chrissie is worried about Kev. He has stopped working at the Norwich Union and taken a job at the furniture store on the corner of St Stephen's roundabout. The store sells discount sofas and king-size beds. Part of Kev's job involves driving a delivery van around the Norfolk countryside, to Dereham, Watton, Garboldisham and Hempnall, but somehow the picturesque villages and the sprawling wheatfields fail to inspire him. In the end they are just like everywhere else, he tells Chrissie. In the cupboard in the spare room, where Kev keeps his fishing tackle, she finds a pile of pornographic magazines. They are far worse than anything you can buy at the newsagent's, and the women in them have knives held to their throats or are trussed up with masking-tape. Kev is shamefaced about the magazines and tells her not to be upset. The baby is born a fortnight later, prematurely, in the back of a taxi taking her to the Norfolk and Norwich Hospital. The story makes the *Eastern Evening News* ('CABBIE'S

UNEXPECTED FARE.') Chrissie is so thankful for the help offered her in the hospital car-park that she finds out the taxi-driver's address and sends him a £10 gift voucher.

The baby is a boy whom they name Keiron. Emma-Jane is fascinated by him and sits for hours by the cot trying to interest him in soft toys and bits of coloured paper. Emma-Jane is going on four now and has Chrissie's mother's sharp eyes and prognathous jaw. Chrissie is besotted by her, so radiantly absorbed that she can scarcely bear to leave her at the nursery school which Emma-Jane attends three mornings a week, pines for the moment when she can wheel Keiron's buggy and bring her back. On one of these excursions they find a dead cat on the stairs with a rip in its side and half its innards spilling out over the concrete. That night Chrissie loses her temper with Kev and says that Mile Cross is no place to bring up children. Kev, back from a hard day's driving along the A14 and away into Cambridgeshire and seeing she is in the right, reluctantly nods his head. It is time to be moving on.

But where to, exactly? Somehow there are fewer places to go in Norwich these days. The council stock is depleting and the right-to-buy properties are filling up with students from the UEA. The local people don't mind the students, although they make too much noise and forget to take their bins in. In London there are riots about the Poll Tax, but Kev says most of the protestors the TV shows dodging the police water cannon don't look as if they've ever paid tax in their life. They spend Kev's twenty-sixth birthday looking at houses in Tuckswood, where the street names are Robin Hood-themed and the pub is called the Maid Marian, but the rents are sky-high and Chrissie doesn't like

the boy-racers who spin round endlessly in their souped-up
Ford Fiestas. In the end, Kev has a bright idea. A friend
of his from the Norwich Union days is taking a security
job in the Gulf, policing some big hotel or other. For a
consideration they can house-sit for him in Wymondham.
It will be the easiest thing, Kev says. All they have to do is
forward the mail and make sure the utility bills get paid,
and Marcus – this is Kev's friend – may not be back for a
couple of years. Chrissie likes the house in Wymondham,
nine miles away along the A11, which is on a new-build
estate and has a fancy washing-machine and a pool table
in the spare room, but there is more building work going
on nearby and the dust aggravates her asthma. One day
in summer when they are having lunch with the window
open she has a coughing fit that won't stop and almost
collapses on the kitchen floor. The doctor prescribes
cortico-steroids, which puff up her face, and tells her to
stay away from the dust.

Kev is sympathetic about the asthma. He is happier here
in Wymondham, Chrissie can see, and says there is more
space. On Saturday afternoons he goes fishing at one of
the local trout lakes and listens to the Norwich game on
the radio. On his way back from one of these excursions,
fossicking around the far side of the estate, he finds a row
of housing association properties, one of which is to let. The
houses are on the small side, but there is a nice patch of
garden where they can have barbecues in summer. Kev has
it all planned. Even better, there is a new primary school
half a mile away where Emma-Jane, who is nearly five, can
go in the autumn. The house is in a close called Heron's
Reach. There are no herons – the adjoining streets have

names like Kingfisher Row and Nuthatch Court – but sometimes on still afternoons you can see a kestrel hovering ominously in the wide, South Norfolk sky.

They stay at Heron's Reach for a long time, all through the '90s and beyond. When Emma-Jane has gone to primary school and Keiron is old enough for nursery, Chrissie takes a part-time job waitressing in a café. It is exhausting work, but the money helps and the regulars – old men poring over the *Mail* and the *Express* and their gossiping wives – are a lively crowd. When Chrissie breaks her wrist coming down on the newly-scrubbed floor, a dozen of them send get-well-soon cards. Kev's new thing is video games. They have names like *Death Squad* and *Armageddon Shoot-out* and occupy him deep into the small hours. Chrissie, tired from her job and dealing with the children, is usually in bed by then, drowsing beneath the big, sprigged coverlet that Kev's parents gave them as a wedding present. Kev is still driving the delivery van for the furniture store, but the work bores him and he is looking for something else. Kev is well into his thirties now, fatter than he used to be and with the beginnings of a bald spot, but, Chrissie can't help noticing, better dressed. He favours crisp little leather jackets, knock-off designer jeans from the market stalls, high-end trainers. Meanwhile, family life is changing. Kev's dad dies and – unexpectedly – leaves him £5,000. They spend nearly half the money on a two-week holiday in Benidorm. Chrissie's Aunty Steph decides to get married again – there have been two previous husbands – and they go over to Shotesham for the wedding, held in an old stone church overlooking a meadow filled with grazing sheep, which Chrissie thinks is the most beautiful thing she has ever seen. Halfway through the ceremony, for no reason she can think of, she bursts into tears and Kev has to take her outside while the children look on, mystified by her distress.

The children are growing up. Emma-Jane is a bulky, raw-boned girl who spends hours watching music programmes on the TV and wants to be a dancer. Keiron, on the other hand, is watchful and nervy, cries if his toys are taken from him and, as far as Chrissie can see, lives off a diet of cornflakes and pasta, Kev – she can tell – is worried about Keiron, tries to teach him to play football on the rec or hauls him off on playdates with his school friend Danny who lives two streets away in Kingfisher Row, but it is never any good. Pete and Amanda, Danny's parents, are friendly people who sometimes invite them round to supper and ask if they want to watch the football on Sky. Pete is some kind of engineer; Amanda works at the Laura Ashley shop in Norwich. Chrissie notices that Kev always puts on a clean shirt when they go round there, slaps some aftershave on his face and is more than usually talkative. Princess Diana dies and they sit watching the endless TV programmes and the mounds of flowers that accumulate in Kensington Gardens. Kev is scornful and says it is what comes of hanging out with Arabs.

Kev, it turns out, has been making plans. Not long after this he tells Chrissie that he is thinking of putting the money left over from his dad's legacy into a vintage clothing stall on Norwich market. He has always been interested in clothes and next month – his informant is Aunty Sheila – one of the stalls will be falling vacant. Amanda has offered to advise him and what does Chrissie think? Privately, Chrissie thinks it is a terrible idea. Kev has always been hopeless with money, and what does he know about vintage clothes? On the other hand, experience has taught her that once he gets an idea in his head there is no stopping him. Kev says he intends to specialise in tee-shirts from the '70s that you can't get anymore and those old high-waisted trousers that Chrissie remembers the kids who went to Northern Soul dances wearing twenty years ago.

The stall is called *Retrovision* and sits halfway along the market's back row, in between a waffle-counter and an old man who sells second-hand books. The clothes come from a warehouse in Salford Amanda has put Kev in touch with and are surprisingly expensive. Kev arranges them on old-fashioned wooden hangers with labels that say *Disco Style* and *Funk Sensations*. The customers are mostly listless teenagers spending their pocket money. Unexpectedly, the stall is a success. A year after it opens they throw a party in the back garden at Heron's Reach whose centrepiece is a cake with RETROVISION picked out in coloured marzipan. It is here, in the small hours, looking out of an upstairs window, while administering a dose of Calpol to the feverish Keiron, that Chrissie sees Kev and Amanda, their heads bent together, sharing a cigarette. Like the last piece of a jigsaw snapping into place, the suspicions that Chrissie has harboured over the past two years are finally explained. Coming downstairs the next morning, she discovers the remains of the cake in the living room, but there is no sign of Kev. When he does return, several hours later, he is shamefaced. It is just a one-off, he tells Chrissie, like the adulterers in the TV soaps, and won't happen again. Chrissie tells him to fuck off. Later she

astonishes herself by stalking round to Kingfisher Row
in the twilight and upending a can of paint over Pete and
Amanda's shiny front door.

The Amanda thing burns on for months. Long before
it ends Chrissie takes the children and decamps to her
mother's. They spend Millennium Night on the sofa in
Colman Road eating pizza and drinking Diet Coke out
of the candy-stripe plastic beakers that have survived from
Chrissie's childhood. Kev is supposed to be living with
Amanda at Heron's Reach. The children take his departure
hard. Emma-Jane, in particular, is always asking after him.
Chrissie's mum says it's an ill wind that blows nobody any
good. She is pushing seventy now and not happy with the
disturbance to her domestic routine. Meanwhile Norwich
is changing. There are black kids in the files of children
heading to CNS and the Hewett in the mornings and the
sub-post office is staffed by a Sri Lankan couple named Mr
and Mrs Goontilleke. For the next three years Chrissie lives
all over the place: in West Earlham, Costessey, Drayton.
There are even two fraught weeks spent in a room above
a pub in Taverham. But somehow they get by. Chrissie
has another job now, in one of the Norwich coffee shops.
It means getting the bus in, but she likes the other women
and sometimes people from the Earlham estate whom she
hasn't seen for twenty years come in and say hello. For some
reason the children don't seem to mind this new lifestyle.
Emma-Jane has stopped wanting to be a dancer and is
taking a hairdressing course at City College. She has a
boyfriend who lives in a bedsit on the Dereham Road with
two wary-looking kids and a vengeful ex who sometimes
leaves furious messages on Emma-Jane's phone. Keiron

is a quiet lad with pale, heavy-lidded eyes, so quiet that Chrissie wonders whether there is something wrong with him. Sometimes at weekends he will sleep 15 hours at a stretch and only wake up when Chrissie yanks the pillow out from under his head. Chrissie adores him and pays £80 for him to go and see a WWF contest at Wembley with a friend and his dad.

The coffee shop manager thinks Chrissie is a good worker and wants to extend her hours. On the strength of this they move into a top-floor flat off the Aylsham Road. It is the kind of place where you wake up in the morning to find the bins kicked over the street, but Chrissie doesn't mind. A fortnight after they move in, the postman delivers a fat, aromatic parcel addressed to the previous tenant that Chrissie is pretty sure is full of weed. The parcel, which sits in the hall for a week, is eventually collected by a silent teenager on a moped. Best to leave that one well alone, Trevor says, who monitors this depredation from the hall-way. Trevor is a tall, nondescript man in his fifties who used to work for the Rowntree Mackintosh factory before they knocked it down and built the Chapelfield shopping mall and has ambitions to be taken on by one of the Timpson's shoe repair shops in the city. Secretly Chrissie thinks he is on the dull side, but she enjoys being treated to the occasional meal or taken on Sunday afternoon trips to the country. Trevor is keen on country houses. Under his auspices they make excursions to Felbrigg, Blickling and Houghton Hall. Chrissie likes the big, spacious gardens, the polished staircases and the portraits of sinewy men in knickerbockers and shooting jackets that hang in the gilt frames, and buys souvenirs – tea towels, jars of exotic

jam – to give to her friends. A tsunami kills thousands of
people in the Far East. Everyone is very excited at Norwich
being back in the Prem.

One Saturday afternoon, out shopping in the city,
Chrissie discovers that the big middle-aged man crossing
the road in front of Jarrold's department store is Kev, and
they stop to talk. Chrissie can see that the fire has gone out
of Kev. He has put on weight and there is something the
matter with his knee that makes his foot bobble slightly on
the kerbside when he walks. But he is so pleased to see her
and so obviously contrite that they end up having coffee
at a nearby Costa. Amanda – Chrissie has heard rumours
of this from the children – is long gone. So, too, is the
market stall, snowed up in a blizzard of unpaid bills and
over-extended credit. Just now Kev is living in a flat-share
off Magdalen Street and working in a mini-market. The
knee is giving him trouble and will probably require an
operation. All in all, Kev says, it has been a bit of a nightmare, and who is this Trevor that the kids have been telling
him about? But Chrissie, kind-hearted even *in absentia*,
will not be drawn on the subject of Trevor. After they have
said goodbye Chrissie watches him stumble off through the
packs of teenagers in from Wymondham and Attleborough
on the bus and the foreign students out shopping for mobile
phones jostling cheerfully on the pavements.

It is a bad winter and the roof in the flat leaks. Trevor
says he has a mate who will come and fix it. Trevor's
world is full of mates who fix things – car-mechanics
and off-duty plumbers and stalwart fence repairers – but
somehow this one never shows. One Sunday afternoon,
out on the Aylsham Road, back from Blickling, Chrissie

tells Trevor that he is the world's most boring man and demands to be driven home. Emma-Jane breaks up with her boyfriend, for reasons that are never satisfactorily explained, and mopes around the flat for a fortnight. Then, in the spring, a woman at the coffee shop tells Chrissie there is a place she knows about on the Earlham estate which the owner wants to let out. The house turns out to be 18 Hodgson Road. Chrissie, inspecting the premises one Sunday afternoon, marvels at the changes that have taken place. Previous owners have stripped the stucco off the bricks and replaced it with plum-coloured render, and the back garden has been sub-divided into a fish-pond and a rockery. With what Emma-Jane is earning, the rent is just about affordable.

They move in on a hot day in 2007. Kev, who has some-how got wind of this, turns up early in the morning with a transit van, for which Chrissie is grateful. The house has been so regularly refurbished in the past twenty years that no trace of their former tenancy seems to survive, but behind one of the radiators, pressed against the wall and crinkling under her hand, Chrissie finds one of the picture-postcards of the Norfolk coast that Kev used to bring home from Jarrold's. The summer burns on. Several of the Bunnett Square shops have changed hands and three of them are charity stores. Emma-Jane is back with her boyfriend and expecting a baby: Chrissie, in a sudden access of fellow-feeling, says that they are welcome to the upstairs back, but that Tyler – this is the name of Emma-Jane's boyfriend – will have to help with the rent. Keiron is at City College three mornings a week and wants to design video games. Sometimes on Friday nights Kev turns up with fish-and-chips or takeaway. It is not quite a settled thing, but Chrissie finds herself quite looking forward to it as Kev can still keep a room full of people entertained with his chat. Kev says he is tired of working at the mini-market and is thinking of driving a cab for Five Star. In the newspapers it says there is a financial crisis in America.

Over at Bacton

Tᴵᴄᴋᴇᴛʏ ʟɪᴠᴇᴅ ᴀᴛ the far end of the Sea Breeze Estate, where the plush houses dwindled away into three-room plasterboard bungalows and lean-to shacks. Calling round that first time with a wheelbarrow full of split logs and eyeing up the ramshackle steps and the smeary windows, he guessed that the next storm would probably take half the roof off. She took a long time to answer the door, but when she did he saw a small woman in corduroys and a denim jacket with a chalk-white face and brindled hair packed up in a bun secured with wooden grips. 'What's that you've got?' she wondered, instantly divining what he, the wheelbarrow and the firewood were doing on the estate on a late-November afternoon when most of the owners had gone back to civilisation and only half-a-dozen of the year-rounders remained.

'Logs,' he told her, and then, somehow sensing that this was no ordinary customer, 'Got a couple of rabbits in the van. Ten pound the pair if you've a mind.'

'I'm good with rabbits,' she said. 'Take them both.'

He didn't like to say that one of the rabbits had been badly chewed up by his dog, but threw in a can of kerosene as a makeweight. Tickety bought a £5 bag of logs as well. Catching a glimpse of the bungalow's sparse interior when she went to fetch the money, he reckoned the bag would probably heat the place for a week. A quarter of a mile away beyond the cliff edge, he could hear the sea booming on the shingle.

'I'll see you again,' he said, stowing the three crinkly five-pound notes away in the back pocket of his jeans.

'I'm always here,' she said, picking up a cat that had strolled out into the doorway and holding it awkwardly in the crook of her arm. 'Don't go anywhere much these days.'

He left her on the doorstep with the cat clamouring to be released and the breeze playing havoc with some wind-chimes that had been fixed to the wooden tracery beneath the kitchen window. For some reason, driving back to North Walsham, the image of her stayed in his head. She would have been about forty, he supposed, and the bungalow had the faintly hippy-ish air he associated with joss sticks, pachouli and dirndl skirts.

'Twenty-five pounds,' his mother said, when he got back and they were eating the sausage and chips he had brought with him. 'Hardly worth going out.'

'There's nothing around, is there?' he complained. 'Blow-ins have all gone back to London after the school half-term. Won't be anyone wanting logs again till Christmas.' A bit later, taking the dog down to the recreation ground, where teenagers smoked cigarettes in the gloaming and threw beer cans at each other, he discovered that he was still thinking about the Sea Breeze Estate, the wind-chimes jingling in the dense air, the sound of the waves booming on the shale and Tickety in her tumbledown doorway.

A week after, despite what he had said to his mother, he found himself on the coast road again, swinging through Walcott and Bacton and slowing down at the village's northern edge to make sure of hitting the turn.

'Don't need any more logs,' Tickety told him. 'Got some coal in. But you're welcome to a cup of tea.'

It was odd, pungent tea that sat heavily in the Union Jack mug and had been over-sugared, but he drank it gratefully.

'What did you do with the rabbit?'

'I made a stew. There's still some left. Why don't you finish it up?'

It was delicious stew, as different from the ones his mother made as a Cromer crab from a jar of fish paste. While he ate it he inspected the room in which they sat, the line of fantasy novels in the bookcase, the batik prints on the wall and the file of miniature elephants that marched across the mantelpiece. Next to the elephants was a red-starred electricity bill addressed to a Mrs Grace Lefebre.

'Don't mind me asking. But why are you called Tickety?'

'It's from when I was a child. I was always asking if things were tickety-boo.'

He stayed until it was nearly dark, mended a catch that had come loose on the back door and worked some putty into a disintegrating window-frame. 'Nice to have a man about the place,' Tickety said. He wondered where the money came from, or if any came at all.

What happened happened gradually. Looking back he could hardly remember the stretch of time that lay in between eating the stew and waking up in the big double bed, with rain falling on the tin roof above their heads and an ominous dripping noise coming from the far side of the room. He fixed the leak in the roof later that morning while Tickety went shopping in Bacton and then started on the grass behind the bungalow. That afternoon they walked along the beach in sight of the gas terminal, and he learned that Tickety had once studied English at Royal Holloway and worked in an art gallery. The intervening years were a blur.

'And what about you?' she said when they were back at the bungalow, drinking more of the black, sweet tea. 'What do you do?'

What did he do? That was a good question, here in North-east Norfolk where many of the traditional patterns of male employment no longer applied. 'I make a living,' he said, which was just about true. Tickety smiled, showing the gaps in her teeth, and he thought that he liked the bungalow and its defective roof and the black tea and the reek of pachouli.

After that they fell into a routine. 'Over at Bacton is it?' his mother would say tolerantly. She was used to this kind of thing. On the other hand, he knew that the new routines needed certain emotional readjustments. 'Heard all about you and your *hippy lady*,' Janice had yelled at him. The North Walsham bush telegraph had been working overtime. 'Why don't you just fuck off somewhere in her gypsy caravan?' He stood on the other side of the bar – Janice worked four nights a week in a pub – gathering his resources for some withering put-down that would make everyone in earshot grin and cackle, but there were no words to say and he knew it.

It was January now, and the population of the Sea Breeze Estate reduced to a hard core of veterans. He had an idea that on the days he didn't call Tickety spent most of her time in bed or hunkered down in front of the fire with her cat reading *The Silmarillion*. Knowing that things like this were always complicated, he wasn't in the least surprised to go round there one afternoon and find a tall, bulky character with a face that looked as if it had been chamfered down with a rasp. 'This is Gary,' Tickety said. Gary gave him a quick, cunning glance, like a fox seen at twilight on the edge of a field. They had some of Tickety's tea – bringing the tray in from the kitchen Gary looked suddenly piratical, as if he had just sailed in from the Spanish Main – and it was all OK, although he could have done without Gary being Tickety's ex-husband. Even less welcome was the news that he had just come out of Norwich Prison.

'What's he been in for?' he asked, after Gary had departed into the night in a beaten-up Ford Escort.

'Extortion, probably.' In Gary's presence Tickety had been a bit less vague and a bit more hard-boiled.

'Where's he staying?'

'Some cunt in Sheringham takes him in, I heard, Gary's all right,' Tickety said. *Gary's all right.* It was what people in this part of Norfolk said about other people less reliable than themselves to whom they wanted to give the benefit of the doubt. The lads from school who had been thrown out for nicking things; the devious shoplifting girls he had known in teendom; his mother's ex-boyfriend, lank and lascivious Maurice: each of them at one time or another had been pronounced *all right*. The North Walsham bush telegraph turned out to know all about Gary. 'You want to watch that one,' his mother advised, like a trainer surveying the line of horses drawn up beneath the starting flag at Great Yarmouth race-track. *What u gonna do now Big Boy back?* Janice texted. None of this inspired confidence, and neither did the handful of flung gravel that bounced off the side of the van as he came driving back from the fish-and-chip shop a couple of nights later. He ignored the figure he could he could see in the tail of one eye as he stepped off the kerb and pressed on into the house, but there were other things that could not be so easily dismissed. 'You lend me £500?' Tickety wondered a couple of days later, as he was upending the latest pile of logs into the bin by the mantelpiece. 'What's it for?' he asked. 'There's always stuff due,' Tickety said, reaching for the fire-tongs, a bit exasperatedly, as if he should have known. 'You can have it back in a week,' she volunteered.

That afternoon they cruised down the A149 as far as Blakeney where the wind was getting up, the boats clanged against each other in the harbour and the walk back to the solitary coffee-shop seemed like the end of the world. It was all falling apart, he thought, and you could see what was going to happen, in the way that the pegged-out cats' cradles of twine on the new-build estates meant a line of houses. Worse, the bait was irresistible. '£400 would do,' Tickety said, raising her head from the half-eaten tea-cake. *'Please.'* All that night he heard Gary in every creak of the floor-boards and every movement the cat made in the other room, but there was no one there.

He raised the money by selling half the logs in the shed off cheap in the pub, taking an armful of old records to the vintage vinyl shop in Cromer and abstracting two £20 notes from the stash his mum kept hidden in the back bedroom's magazine stack, suspecting all the while that it would do no good. The Ticketys of this world always escaped from the nets flung out to pinion them. Worse, they could drag you to drown at their side. Turning up at the estate two days later, with the £400 safe in an envelope on the dashboard, he discovered two police cars parked up outside the bungalow and the glass gone from the front window. Gary, sitting in the back seat of the second car and looking more piratical than ever, was fending off questions from a policewoman. There was no sign of Tickety.

He gave it a week before going back – time enough for order to be restored and the source of trouble to be rooted out – but the place was just as he had left it: the door half-open and the smashed glass still strewn over the wooden steps; the tracks the police cars had made still disfiguring the broken turf. A bit later the cat came slinking round the side of the house, fur stiff in the breeze, and he knelt down and made encouraging noises, but the cat was an old enemy and went back the way it had come. Wanting a souvenir, he unhitched the wind-chimes from the wooden trellis beneath the gaping window and put them in his jacket pocket, thinking about Tickety's white face, the boats at Blakeney and the gunmetal sky edging away beyond them.

At Mr McAllister's

'I'VE ORDERED A dozen of those new Fieseler Storch kits the Airfix rep was talking about last week.'

'That sounds about right,' Jason said. He did not know what a Fieseler Storch was, but it was good to be kept in the loop.

'That chap in the RAF tie who comes in on Saturday mornings will buy two, you mark my words. He likes that sort of thing. I've only signed up for six of the Sopwith Camel Dogfight Doubles,' Mr McAllister went on. 'People don't seem so interested in the Great War stuff.'

'I'm sure that will be enough.'

'They've paired it with the Fokker triplane.' Mr McAllister's face had assumed the intent, serious expression that he brought to discussions of his professional calling. 'I've a good mind to try making one myself.'

The shop lay halfway along the Royal Arcade, in sight of Gentleman's Walk and the first few market stalls, squeezed between a genteel tea parlour and an interior decorator's showroom. The sign over the door said 'Toys for Boys', but the shop's official name was 'McAllister's Model Emporium.' As well as supplying model aircraft kits and facsimiles of antique sailing ships, it sold boxes of 00-scale toy soldiers, Action Men and back numbers of *Commando* magazine. There was an upstairs room where microscopes gathered dust in display cases and war-gaming societies sometimes held meetings, but this was not much visited.

'There's quite a lot you can be getting on with this morning,' Mr McAllister said doggedly. 'No one's ever going to buy those lunar landing craft. They're just taking up valuable space. So I want you to box them up and send them back. Say they're damaged stock or something. Ask for a full refund. After that there's the dusting to do. And then it's time someone had a go at the window display. That model of Ice Planet Hoth's been there since the film came out.'

'Quite a lot of demand,' Jason countered. 'For the *Star Wars* stuff, I mean.'

'Ah, but it's not proper modelling is it?' Mr McAllister said. 'Just a fad for the kids. I mean, none of the serious collectors would be seen dead buying a kit of Chewbacca or whatever his name is.' Mr McAllister was a short, solid man of about fifty with sparse, Brylcreemed hair parted in the middle whose outlook on life had, as he often said, been transformed by doing National Service in the Army Catering Corps. In an ideal world he would have liked to sell nothing but aircraft models from the two world wars, but he was enough of a businessman to realise that temporary aberrations in the trade had to be allowed to run their course.

'So,' he said, in summary, 'that's returns, dusting and Ice Planet Hoth. If you've a spare moment you could pop over to Tracy's and get that Hoover back I lent her last week. That's if she hasn't burnt out the motor.'

After that Mr McAllister put on his Harrington over-coat and a pair of wash-leather gloves and went off to the bank, leaving Jason in the tiny space carved out between a head-high pile of B17 Flying Fortresses and some assorted 'Figures from History' which would very soon go the same way as the lunar landing craft. He was a tall, pale boy of eighteen who for some reason hadn't liked working at the Norwich Union Insurance Society, and so his father, who knew Mr McAllister through the Freemasons, had fixed him up with the model shop.

Slowly the January morning passed. A teenager in a bright blue blazer who was clearly bunking off school came in and bought an Avro 504K Tiger Moth kit, closely followed by a crop-haired man in a bomber jacket who wanted to complain about some missing parts in a Lancaster kit his wife had given him for his birthday. The shop's clientele fell into three strictly demarcated categories: small boys spending their pocket-money; your middle-aged hobbyists and women buying presents for their menfolk. There were friends of Mr McAllister who had lofts full of unopened boxes bought as an investment to be cashed in at some remote point in the future when shares in obscure Nazi spy-planes were at a premium.

Mr McAllister was late coming back and claimed to have been held up by a dispute over a bounced cheque. On the other hand, he also smelt of beer. Rocking on his heels just inside the doorway, a tightly-furled copy of the *Daily Telegraph* sticking out of his coat-pocket, he said: 'Don't forget I shall need you for the Aeromodellers' Club this evening. There's about twenty of them supposed to be coming. Your father said you wouldn't mind.'

'I hadn't forgotten,' Jason assured him. The Aeromodellers' Club met in the upstairs room twice a month and needed to be closely supervised. Mr McAllister took off the coat with a certain amount of difficulty and put a bag of crisps and a pork pie on the counter, which was a signal that Jason could take his lunch break. Jason collected his Parka jacket and the Tupperware box which contained his sandwiches and went off in the direction of the market, hoping to see the exceptionally pretty girl who worked on one of the fruit and vegetable stalls or the man who assured the impressionable housewives to whom he sold handbags that they were pure python and he knew this because had been down to Caister and shot them. However, the handbag stall was shut up and the pretty girl who sold fruit and vegetables was having a furious argument with a boy in a leather jacket, and so he walked through the market and up the steps on the further side and ate his sandwiches on a bench in the shadow of the war memorial. When he came back a new consignment of stock had arrived and Mr McAllister was sitting cross-legged on the floor surrounded by boxes of Halifax bomber kits.

'Flew in one of those once,' he said, tapping his hand to his forehead in a mock salute. 'Never forget that climb up the steps. Gives you a feeling like nothing else in life.'

◊

'We need to rethink this,' Mr McAllister said the next

morning. He had had his hair cut in a new way that had
the effect of emphasising how little of it there was left.

'What do we need to rethink?' Jason asked.

'This,' Mr McAllister said, sweeping his hand high
above his head in a gesture that took in everything from
the window-display to a stack of Hornby trains that was
blocking up the doorway, 'All of it.'

The Aeromodellers' Club meeting had not been a
success. Theoretically they were supposed to drink cups
of tea, eat the tray of buns that Jason had brought in from
the baker's shop at the Back of the Inns and buy items of
stock. Instead they had spent most of the time arguing
about how you painted the undercarriage of a Blenheim
night-fighter that was under construction.

'It's all going napoo,' Mr McAllister said, who liked
using old-fashioned military slang 'The last six months'
figures are terrible. I've been speaking to Gerda about it.
She's got some ideas. She's going to come in later and talk
about it.'

Although he was unmarried and puritanical by nature,
Mr McAllister was surprisingly interested in the opposite
sex. Gerda, on the other hand, was different from most of
the meek local women whom Jason had previously seen
him with. She was a tall, well-made lady in her early forties
who spoke excellent, if stilted English in a pronounced
German accent, was supposed to have once worked for
a toy company and had met Mr McAllister at a trade
convention.

'For a start,' Mr McAllister said – he had fallen down
on one knee, the better to examine the lower layers of the
stock – 'we're going to get rid of some unprofitable lines. I

mean, nobody makes railways anymore. It's like fretwork or keeping cage birds. Gone out completely. Take you, now. What are you? Eighteen? What do your friends do in their spare time?'

This was a futile question. Jason knew that what his friends did in their spare time would have appalled Mr McAllister. So he said: 'They go to football matches. And they listen to music.'

'My point exactly,' Mr McAllister said. The high-spiritedness he had brought to the proposed culling of unprofitable lines was shading into his usual bedrock pessimism. 'We need to go where the money is.'

Gerda arrived in the dull late-morning period, before the swarms of shop workers and insurance clerks were let out for their lunch-hours. She was wearing an expansive fur-coat and the clack of her high heels on the polished floor of the arcade could be heard for several seconds before she came into the shop. Mr McAllister, deep in conversation with a crony who claimed to have been in the French Foreign Legion, waved at her eagerly and then went back to talking about Algeria and the *pied noirs*.

'How are you, Jason?' Gerda asked in a motherly way. Up close she smelled of face-cream and Parma Violets. 'You know, a boy your age should not be working in a place like this. Surrounded by all this . . .' – a Messerschmidt ME109 hung from a wire just above her head and her eye fell on it – '. . . *militaria*. You should be at a university or a college of further education. You should wish to better yourself.'

Jason never knew quite how seriously these remarks were meant to be taken. But he liked Gerda and welcomed her interest in him.

'Would you like a cup of tea, Mrs Mannerheim?'

'You are a polite boy, Jason.' The beam of Gerda's smile was quite paralysing, like a lamp coming on in a darkened street. 'But you take formality too far. You must call me Gerda.'

The man who said he had been in the French Foreign Legion was eventually persuaded to leave the shop, having bought a model of a Lockheed Hudson and six tins of Humbrol paint. Mr McAllister and Gerda looked conspiratorially at each other, went upstairs and began to racket around. Jason tried to follow their conversation and then lost interest and went back to rearranging the window display with its line of Wellingtons being menaced by Stuka dive-bombers. He had a feeling, which he disliked, that change was afoot. A bit later a rep came into the shop and tried to interest him in some more Star Wars figures. Mr McAllister and Gerda were gone a long time. Once or twice he heard the noise of boxes being shifted about and things falling onto the floor. Presently Gerda came slowly down the staircase, placing the points of her heels carefully between the runners.

'Progress has been made,' she declared, not quite triumphantly. 'Ernest' – this was Mr McAllister's Christian name – 'says he will soon be taking you on a little excursion. I shall be interested in your opinion.' Her gaze returned to the ME109. 'You know, my father flew in one of these machines? It was not something he ever cared to speak of. After that he became a teacher of the sciences. It was a hard life, but a successful one.'

There was no knowing what to make of this. Mr McAllister, thumping downstairs a moment or two after she had gone with strands of hair uncoiling from the top of his head, looked odder than ever. Jason wondered if he was about to lose his temper about something: this happened about every six weeks and was always interesting to watch. He had a sudden vision of Mr McAllister, alone in the house he was supposed to inhabit at Thorpe End, brewing himself cups of Camp Coffee and listening to cassette tapes of *The Navy Lark*.

'After lunch I've got a little trip planned for us,' Mr McAllister said, mysteriously. 'Make sure you're back in time.'

He took his packed lunch up to the market again, walking determinedly through the shoals of schoolchildren and the middle-aged men in car coats who stood around smoking cigarettes and slapping their hands against their sides to ward off the cold. The pretty girl on the fruit and vegetable stall gave him a glance that was not exactly contemptuous but implied that he was a feeble specimen over whom tough boys in leather jackets, however quarrelsome, would always have the edge. She was what his mother would have called 'a bit common-looking', but this did not lessen her allure. Back at the shop, Mr McAllister had grown brisk and purposeful and was standing just inside the door with the piece of card that said 'Back in Ten Minutes' on it.

'Anything happen at the market?'

'The man who sells the handbags had got a new consignment in. It was quite funny.'

'I dare say it was,' Mr McAllister said.

The excursion turned out to be taking them only a few yards away along Gentleman's Walk to Jarrold's department store. This was enemy territory, but Mr McAllister seemed to know what he was doing. Silently they made their way up to the third floor, where the toys lay in limitless profusion, row upon row, as far as the eye could see. As a child Jason had spent long hours here staring at the files of Napoleonic soldiery in their display cases and the regiments of Action Men lined up in their brightly-coloured cardboard boxes. A decade later he was aware that his loyalty was wanted elsewhere. But Mr McAllister showed no interest in such parts of the Jarrold stock that duplicated his own.

'This is what we're looking for,' he said.

The bears had been arranged in a giant wall of artificial fur. They had names like Tenderheart Bear and Birthday Bear and were quite expensively priced. As they stood watching, a small girl ran out of the surrounding crowd and pulled one from the stack.

'You can't go wrong with this kind of thing,' Mr McAllister said. He picked up one of the bears, held it up in front of him and then drew it close to his face as if he were about to give it some important advice. 'Decent margins, too.'

A bit later they went back down the staircase, past the magazine stall and the perfume counter and out into the street. Something seemed to strike Mr McAllister and he said:

'Did your father ever get into Rose Croix?'

Jason knew that this had something to do with Freemasonry. 'I think he did.'

'It's more than I managed,' Mr McAllister said gloomily, 'But then I've enough on my plate as it is.'

◊

The changes to the shop took place incrementally. It did
not do, Mr McAllister said, to rush into things. A space
was cleared for the Care Bears on the left-hand side of the
till; the stock of model trains was returned to the manu-
facturers and the Aeromodellers' Club was told that it
would have to find other premises. All this, as Jason could
see, made Mr McAllister restless. When not supervising
the new arrangements he took long lunch-hours or went
poking around in odd corners, moving boxes from one
part of the shop to another and then putting them back.
The bears sold well without making a dramatic impact
on Mr McAllister's finances. It was early February now,
with snow on the ground, so that the customers wore thick
coats and Wellington boots that left runnels of dirty water
oozing over the floor. 'Nasty times,' Gerda said, who had
been deputed to mind the shop on the Monday when Mr
McAllister was away at the Earl's Court Toy Fair, 'but
we can amuse ourselves, you and I, and have everything
looking ship-shape and in Bristol fashion.' They amused
themselves by dusting the microscope cabinets, which
Gerda said would have to go, and coming across a pile of
Meccano magazines dating from the early 1960s.

Early in the afternoon it began to snow again and the
flow of customers dwindled to one every fifteen minutes.
'And now,' Gerda said, 'we must reorganize the window.'
For the purposes of rearranging the shop she had changed
into a suit of blue overalls and tied a bright red handker-
chief over her ash-blonde hair. 'We must reorganise the
windows and make a surprise for Ernest when he comes

home.' Jason realised – something that he had not quite understood before – that he was mesmerised by Gerda, that she held him entirely in her thrall, and that – like the girl on the market stall – he would have done more or less anything she asked him to do. Under her direction he began to take the boxes of Messerschmidt 262As and Heinkel bombers, slim, pencil-shaped Dorniers of the kind that his grandmother had once seen out of an upstairs window of the family house in 1942, and stacked them up next to the door. Gerda looked on approvingly.

'We shall make some changes here,' she said. 'We shall make some big changes.'

'Which squadron did your father fly in?' Jason asked.

'I do not recollect. It is not important,' Gerda said, kicking several boxes of RAF Lysanders further in the direction of the counter, and he saw that it had been the wrong thing to say.

Mr McAllister, coming back unexpectedly early from Toy Fair, did not at first seem to understand what was going on. He stood in the middle of the shop, in a space that had opened up between the reconditioned boxes, and hovered there with his hands in his pockets looking at them in a puzzled way.

'What have you done?' he demanded in the end. 'Why have you done this?'

'You are not to get on your high horse,' Gerda told him. It is necessary that we take this step. You will thank me for it.'

'Why have you done it? You know we talked about this.' For a moment there was a wheedling tone in his voice. Then he brought his foot down heavily on the floor.

'Why have you taken all the things out of the window?'

'We have had this conversation many times,' Gerda said, with a certain amount of weariness. 'Many times we have had it.'

But Mr McAllister knew, or thought he knew, why the boxes had been taken out of the window.

'Look,' he said brokenly. 'Look here. You can't do this. We won the war, you know.'

Jason decided to leave them to it. A moment or two later, well wrapped up in his Parka, he made his way along the Arcade, pursued by the sound of their raised voices. Here in Gentleman's Walk the street lamps were coming on and the market traders were starting to pack up their stalls. Someone had spilled a crate of apples open on the pavement, and he picked one up and ate it as he walked.

◊

Nothing was said the next morning about what had happened the previous afternoon. On the other hand, all the boxes had been put back in the window and the Care Bears had gone from their vantage point next to the counter. Going into the room at the back of the shop to make their mid-morning coffee, he discovered the severed head of one sitting on top of the overflowing wastepaper basket.

'Did I tell you,' Mr McAllister said, shortly after this, 'that I'm letting the Aeromodellers have their meeting here again? Apparently they couldn't find anywhere else to go. I thought it would be for the best.'

'I'm sure you're right,' Jason said.

That lunchtime he took his box of sandwiches up to

the big library next to the City Hall and stood looking at the display of municipal advertisements. There was one about studying for your A-Levels at the City College, and he fished out a Biro that had got stuck in the lining of his jacket and wrote down the details on the back of his hand. Hastening back through the market, past the shack selling cut-price jeans and the old man who repaired watches, he came in sight of the fruit and vegetable stall. For perhaps the first time in his experience the girl who worked there was disengaged, neither selling produce nor arguing with tough boys in leather jackets, but simply standing there, rapt and observant, behind a tray of bananas and adjusting the bobble hat she wore on cold days with a guileless hand. Driven by some impulse he could barely fathom, and not in the least knowing what would be the result of it, he started to walk towards her.

The Methwold Kid

THE CHITTOCKS WERE farming people who had lived in Methwold – which they called *Methuld* – for long enough to take themselves seriously and be so taken. When the farm went, to an agribusiness for less than everyone expected, they drifted off into inferior trades, drove delivery vans out over the Breckland flat, put up fences or tenanted market stalls in Swaffham. There was no shame in this as they had managed to keep the big farmhouse on the edge of the wheat-fields and a little of the status that went with it. All the same their numbers were declining, and by the time the early 2000s rolled into view there was only old Mrs Chittock and her grown-up son Horace living in the farmhouse and a couple of married sisters and their families quartered on a newbuild estate Watton way, all of them subsidised by a fair amount of money in the bank and a pious hope that the future would look after itself.

Horace was fifty now, cragged up – all the male Chittocks went this way eventually – short-tempered but biddable. If there was time standing spare, then he filled it by taking his mother to her hospital appointments or picking through the rusted car-parts that cluttered up the yard. No one had ever thought it incongruous that he and the old lady ate their supper in a faded dining room with photographs of distant ancestors and fenland scenes on the wall and that the soup was served out of a tureen with Queen Victoria's portrait on the lid: that was how things went on out here in the Brecks, where modernity was kept at bay and the GP declining to call but requesting attendance at the surgery was taken as a personal insult. Jemima's arrival, too, might have been taken as a mark of how things went on, part of a rhythm, a dance where the steps were pre-ordained and the music never stopped. It seemed that one moment she and Horace were trading small-talk in Swaffham high street and the next they were standing outside the church porch with a friend holding up a golf umbrella against the spray of spring drizzle. It was a proper Methwold wedding, with the honeymoon postponed until summer, and then let go indefinitely, bells tied to the mattress and drinking until dawn. Next morning there were still a dozen guests asleep in the front room for Horace to make tea for when he staggered downstairs.

Jemima was thirty-five, sharp-faced and calculating but tolerant of Horace and his foibles. Until her marriage she had driven round the locale cutting people's hair in their front rooms. Now she was keen to make hay. Mrs Chittock disliked her daughter-in-law from the start on account of her being from Garboldisham and a Nightingale, a family which the Chittocks had never held in high regard. 'She'll be a-slinking round the place currying favour,' she warned Horace. When Jemima had given her a beauty salon token as a present that first Christmas she was unimpressed. 'I'm too old for this sort of thing and she ought to know,' she

complained. But it was Jemima who set Horace's new life
– if that is what it was – in motion. To her the handyman's
skills he had been taught as a boy were a marketable asset.
'There is money to be made out there, Hor,' she explained.
'Gravelling up people's drives and seeing to the gutters.
Property management, they call it. You get in there and
see if there's some for you.'

To his surprise, Horace found that she was right. The
western edge of Norfolk seemed to be full of houses needing work. Overgrown gardens and pot-holed driveways
weren't the half of it. The commissions Horace couldn't
execute himself he sub-contracted out. Most of the houses
were owned by people new to the area – from London,
Birmingham, places even further adrift – but Horace
wasn't one of the Methwold diehards who shuddered every
time they heard an alien accent. He was happy to take
their money, and even happier when he discovered they
had no idea of how much things ought to cost. You could
charge some wide-eyed second-homer £1,000 to repoint
one of his side-walls and freshen up the concrete on his
terrace and he'd write the cheque on the spot. In this way
the business prospered. In a year Horace had a van with
H. CHITTOCK PROPERTY MAINTENANCE
AND SECURITY SERVICES stencilled on the side,
a couple of leaf-blowers and a boy called Moby Stannard
to climb up trees and help him with the lifting.

'Your missus have got you properly sorted,' his friend
Heck Barr volunteered one night when they were out
pubbing, which might have been meant as a compliment
but caused Horace to take issue. 'You could say that,' he
said. 'Time someone got you properly sorted' – Heck, who

drained out tempest-sodden ditches for the council, had never aspired to a van. 'Ah, you're the Methwold Kid,' Heck said, which was what they used to yell at each other – it was something to do with the Milky Bar ads you saw on the TV – forty years ago. Driving back home with four pints of Woodforde's Wherry inside him and keeping a wary eye on the curves of the country roads, Horace reflected that it was true. Even better, Jemima's managerial skills extended to the farmhouse, where the meals were invariably on time, the shirts came ironed and there was talk of foreign holidays. 'I'm not saying she can't cook or lay a table,' Mrs Chittock remarked, when Horace pointed out some of these refinements. 'But them Nightingales never had no pride. She'll let you down, and when she does you'll know about it. And seeing as we're talking, two of your grandma's gold pins are gone from the box upstairs.' The gold pins turned up in an envelope on the kitchen dresser, but Horace knew it wasn't going to end there. Nothing did in this part of Norfolk, where people cut dependents from their wills on a whim, stalked out of family meals on Christmas Day and left clan feuds bubbling on for their grandchildren to settle half-a-century later.

Was it Jemima who told him about the Mountfields? Afterwards Horace couldn't remember. There were five of them: a man in his mid-fifties; corn-haired glamour wife a year or two younger; two skinny grown-up sons who came and went – students, Horace reckoned – and an old mum who drove erratically round the lanes in a Fiat Panda clipping hedges and pasting pheasants into the tarmac. The big house on the edge of town had all the things needing done to it that such properties usually required: hedges trimming; moles routed out from under the lawn; defective gutters sealing – things that many a self-respecting house-holder could have fixed himself, Horace thought as he and Moby sped up the driveway that first time. Still, unlike most of the second-homers, the Mountfields turned out to be affable and confiding. Agnetha, who was Swedish, reminded Horace of her namesake in Abba. There was something familiar about the husband, Rob, as well – so familiar that Horace found himself sneaking glances at him, trying to coax some long-buried memory back to the surface of his mind. As well as being affable and confiding, the Mountfields were also free-spending, paid up the £1500 invoice Horace cheerfully submitted for the lawn without turning a hair and presented him with a brace of pheas-ants out of a crammed deep-freezer. The pheasants were plucked and came from the game shop in Meth, whereas Horace preferred them feathered and shot by himself, but he appreciated the gesture.

After that the Mountfields started to turn up regularly: like the lines of teal that rose off the fields at dawn and flew off over the border into Cambridgeshire. Agnetha was supposed to have cleared out the meat counter at a nearby farm shop in one fell swoop. They came to the pub on charity night and bought £100-worth of tickets. Heck Barr, swiftly introduced to the supply chain, billed them £1200 for a set of garden-steps that any amateur carpenter could have knocked into place in an hour and a half. Delivering a couple of bags of salt for the water-softener one autumn afternoon, Horace found himself welcomed into a big converted garage where a wall of computers beamed out stock prices from around the globe. He was semi-retired really, Rob conceded, but liked to keep his hand in. Not long after that the reason why he looked so familiar fell out.

'Had my suspicions when we first came here,' he told Horace one lunch-time in the unruly meadow that the Mountfields called a paddock, 'but now I know. I reckon you and me are family.'

'That so?' Horace queried. He was looking at the fence-posts at the field's farther end and wondering if they needed replacing.

'Didn't your dad have a cousin called Annie Sycamore? Well, that's my mother.'

Horace had heard of the Sycamores, just about: the Chittocks were not great ones for keeping in touch. His own mother found the photo of Billy Sycamore, Annie's brother, and detected a resemblance in the pale, high forehead and the swept-aside features. It was Mrs Chittock, too, who divulged why the families had fallen apart. 'Two cottages over at Feltwell,' she explained. 'Should have been something in writing, but there wasn't. Sold up after your granddad died and nobody said a word. Your father wouldn't ever talk to him after that. Came over one Christmas and he shut the door in his face.' All this, Horace knew, went with the territory. It was how people behaved round here: the hills on which they took their stand. Several of the fence-posts were indeed found to be rotting, or near enough, and Horace and Heck eagerly set about their repair. 'And another thing,' Mrs Chittock complained. 'That silver-plated hair-band have gone.'

There were other similarities beyond the high forehead and the swept-aside features. Rob, Horace noticed, had his father's thick, spatulate fingers. Watching them write the cheque for the new fence-posts – £600 seemed a fair price – he could have been back in the farmhouse thirty years ago with his dad volunteering to subsidize the Garelli motorcycle that had so nearly brought him to grief once out on the back-lanes when a partridge had skittered out under the front wheel and he'd gone over onto the verge. Unexpectedly, the memory cheered him, the old world suddenly raising its head above a tide of modern rubbish. Not long after that Rob asked: did he ever go fishing, and Horace was able to put him in the way of a members-only trout lake. They spent a complicit afternoon or two, Horace smiling at the fancy creel and high-end rods that Rob unloaded from his Range Rover, but enjoying the solidarity of the two middle-aged cousins side by side at the water's edge and the deference in Rob's voice as he asked about lures and bread-paste bait.

He got back to find his mother asleep in a chair and Jemima briskly up-ending a pile of chopped parsnips into a Le Creuset casserole pot.

'That Agnetha was round here this afternoon,' she began, with surprising brusqueness 'Wanted to fix up some cleaning work.'

There were times when Horace was slow off the mark. 'Well, we could sort that,' he said, thinking of Heck's wife, the notoriously under-employed Becka Barr.

'You're not getting it. She asked if I'd go and clean their house. Two mornings a week.'

'I am getting it. She wants *you* to clean *her* house.'

'Now look here, Hor,' Jemma temporised, seeing the look in his eye. 'Isn't any harm in thinking about it. Don't reckon she meant any offence. Was just trying to be friendly if you ask me.'

'I didn't ask you,' Horace said. He had been betrayed many times in his life, by women, weather, football teams and horses. But this was a throwing-over of a different order. Due at the Mountfields the next morning to inspect some under-nourished grass on the front lawn, he voted to stay at home. When Rob phoned the following day, polite and solicitous and wondering if there were anything wrong, he slammed the receiver angrily down in its cradle. And there the matter might have rested for a while, had they not bumped into each other in Meth high street. 'Done something to offend you, mate?' Rob said in that puzzled way Horace had always associated with his father. He was carrying a sanding machine from the local hardware store that must have cost £500. For a moment Horace regretted the fact that he and Heck would never have the opportunity to instruct him in its use. 'Need to show some respect, you do,' Horace yelled as he passed, and then, over his shoulder, 'you and your swindling old uncle.' Walking back to the van, he couldn't quite decide if he was proud of himself, half-ashamed or the victim of some quite different emotion, precariously balanced between the two. That night Mrs Chittock ran the vanished hair-band to earth in Jemima's handbag.

Drowning in Hunny

'THIS IS A funny place and no mistake,' Mr Benefer said, one hand scratching at the few grey curls that still ornamented the back of his head, the other slapping feebly at a wasp that was crawling over the plate-glass counter. 'I mean, did you know there are three separate names for it? That's right.' Mr Benefer had lost interest in the wasp, which was buzzing with impunity over a brass tray piled high with sugar-mice. 'Standard pronunciation *Hun-stan-ton* in three syllables. But posh types – you know, the King when he comes down from Sandringham of a morning – call it *Hunston*. Hunston? Can you imagine that?' His face, shiny and wind-raked from a day out in the summer sun and now framed by the shop's pink and grey interior, looked indescribably odd. 'And then there are divots out in the swamps who call it *Hunny*. Not that it's anything to do with me,' Mr Benefer said hastily, as if several representatives of Hunstanton Town Council stood waiting outside to rebuke this incautious remark. 'I'm just here to sell them things.'

Alex, who knew that he was one of the divots who called it Hunny, decided not to say anything. After three months in the shop, he was aware that there were times when Mr Benefer needed to be given his head and that this was one of them.

'Anyway, I'll leave that to finer minds than mine,' Mr Benefer went on, with a dreadful satirical laugh. A teenage boy with absurdly over-developed biceps in a Rage Against the Machine tee-shirt came into the shop and Mr Benefer shot him a look of such fathomless hostility that he turned on his heel and went out again. 'Lots to do today, what with the school holidays starting and all the kids coming in. I shall want you to shift all those crates out of the chiller, and it's time someone went through all the shrimping nets we had left over from last year and stapled up the holes, which I can tell you is a tricky job.'

Outside there was more bright sun streaming over the esplanade and glittering off the nearby sea. One or two boats were plying back and forth and a ribbon of surf over in the corner tracked the path of a solitary jet-skier. Otherwise there was no one much about. The air, as was usual at this time of day, smelled of salt, cooking oil, fish and burnt sugar from the candy-floss concern three doors down.

'And you'd better count all those toy umbrellas,' Mr Benefer said. 'I was told there were two dozen, but it looks a lot less.'

The shop sold confectionery, soft drinks, sandwiches from a refrigerator cabinet and a wide range of holiday-maker's requisites. The display case at the far end was an undifferentiated mass of flip-flops, buckets, plastic spades and picnic-ware. Next to it stood a teetering spindle of postcards with views of North Norfolk. Mr Benefer was the third tenant in five years and there were times, Alex thought, when his employer's heart was not in it.

'10.32,' Mr Benefer said, holding his watch an inch or two from his face like a character in a comedy film. 'Where the *fuck* has that smackhead got to?'

This was unfair on Marcus, who rarely took anything stronger than weed, but it was the kind of thing Mr Benefer said. He had once referred to his fellow-tradesmen as 'a crowd of sugar-sanding, treacle-watering, shit-stabbing grocers.'

'I've got to go out,' Mr Benefer said, whose fundamental restlessness could only be appeased by leaving the shop half-a-dozen times a day and walking furiously up and down the esplanade. 'When he gets here, tell him I expect him to do everything I've told you and no shirking. And tell him I'm docking an hour and fifteen minutes off his pay.'

'I'll do that,' Alex said, only to find that Mr Benefer had already left the shop and was plunging away up the slight incline that lay at an acute angle beyond it. Clenched fists bunched against his torso, the remnants of his grey hair unravelling in the breeze, he looked a man possessed. In his absence the interior of the shop seemed to calm down, become cooler and more inviting and yet at the same time diminished by the removal of its authenticating force. Alex's three seasons' worth of summer holiday jobs in Hunstanton had taken in an ice-cream parlour, a pie-shop and a stint at the Tourist Information Office, but they had never previously turned up anyone like Mr Benefer.

'Has that fat fuck gone out again?' Marcus said, materialising so rapidly in front of the counter that it was as if he had sprung up out of the ground. He was good at

timing his entrances to coincide with Mr Benefer's exits.
Sometimes whole days went by without their setting eyes
on each other. 'I saw him walking along the front yesterday
and he looked practically insane. They're bound to lock
him up soon, don't you think?'

Like Mr Benefer, Marcus was not from these parts.
He was a tall, confident boy a year older than Marcus
with a degree in Slavonic Studies and what Alex's mother
would have called a 'half-crown voice', and his presence
in Mr Benefer's shop, or indeed in Hunstanton itself, was
inexplicable.

'Get sacked you will, going on like that,' Alex said
admiringly. 'He catches you saying things like that, you'll
be out on your ear.'

'No I won't. Benefer loves me. If he cuts up rough I can
charm him down from the trees. You'll see.'

Curiously enough, this was very nearly true. Though he
groused constantly about Marcus, stood ostentatiously in
the doorway looking out for him when he was late for work
and was always docking his pay for minor infringements
of the shop's disciplinary code, deep down Mr Benefer was
entirely smitten by him and had once presented him with
a cheap bottle of sherry.

'Benefer,' Marcus said, springing two tins of Coke from
the fridge and twisting off their ring-pulls, 'Benefer can eat
my dust. Now, have I told you about Martha?'

'No. Who's she?' Marcus was always talking about girls
he had met in unusual circumstances, so regularly that it
was sometimes difficult to know whether they existed or
not.

'I don't know. I suppose you'd call her a hippy chick.

She's staying at one of the camp-sites. I'm meeting her for a drink after work. Why don't you come along?'

Deeply gratified but taking care not to show it, Alex said that he would. Seeing that there was no sign of Mr Benefer coming back, they drank the Cokes, pilfered some bags of crisps and then started taking the crates out of the chiller. At intervals people came into the shop to buy snacks, but the flip-flops, spades, buckets and picnic-ware lay neglected in the display cases. Then, when the mid-day traffic had died down, Marcus shook out a box of Swan Vestas and wrote the words BENEFER IS A DICK in match-stalks on the counter. This was generally how they spent the time here in Mr Benefer's shop, in Hunstanton, on long summer mornings in the school holidays when he was out walking.

◊

Against considerable odds, Martha turned out to exist. She was a short, squat girl in a ballooning dress and gypsy ear-rings who drank three pints of snakebite without obvious ill-effects and talked in a desultory way about some goats she was trying to raise on a smallholding in Lincolnshire. What Marcus could see in her, or she in him, Alex couldn't fathom. On the other hand, did people need to see anything in anyone, or have that interest returned? Alex was used to low-level relationships, inches given and received, getting on and getting by. There was no point in tormenting yourself. When Marcus arrived next morning at 11.05, to a shop thronged with obstreperous vacationing children, Mr Benefer said: 'You're treading on thin ice, Marky-boy. Do that again and it's the order of the bowler hat.' It was extraordinary where Mr Benefer got these pieces of bygone slang. 'Oh come on Mr B,' Marcus said, flashing his splendid teeth in a craven smile. 'You know you wouldn't do that. Why cast aside the one thing in your otherwise humdrum life that gives it savour?' And for some reason Mr Benefer bridled, as at the wildest compliment. That day, despite the increased traffic of the shop, he went out for more walks than he had ever been known to take and gave them both free tickets to the Aquarium. 'I don't *think* he's gay,' Marcus said. 'At the same time I don't think I'd like to be left alone in a darkened room with him.'

The summer was getting on now. The holidaymakers came in waves. Just as you had got used to one lot of them they briskly dispersed and another cargo arrived. Martha went back to Lincolnshire and her goats and was replaced by a girl called Alice who wore Goth paraphernalia even in August but was apparently a marchioness's great-niece. On days off, or on afternoons when Mr Benefer decided to shut up the shop and go to Yarmouth races, they went racketing up the coast beyond Heacham, to the point where the holiday villages gave out and there was only sand, sea and the great wide sky, sat on the shingle, drank beer out of tins and threw stones at the rocks. 'How long have you been doing this?' Marcus enquired on one of these excursions, meaning summer holiday work, and Alex owned up to his three seasons selling pies and advising people who came to the Tourist Information Centre of the best way to get to Sandringham. He could still not work Marcus out, but somehow the working-out seemed incidental to it all, the strew of beer-cans on the beach and Alice's clumpy boots and overwrought eyeliner. A sedate life, but not without its advantages. At Heacham once they stood and watched as an old man who had had a heart attack was worked over by a pair of paramedics ferried in by the air ambulance. A week after this Marcus invited him to a party at a big house near Burnham Market, which, although nothing was said, Alex surmised might belong to one of Marcus's relatives, and reinforced the mystery of what he was doing in Mr Benefer's shop. 'It's a very odd thing,' he overheard Alice say as the stragglers convened the next morning in a basement kitchen and somebody wondered about boiling up a lump of cod from the freezer, 'but the Queen doesn't have fish-knives.'

And with the summer's advance came evidence of people's plans and stratagems: the ceramics course Alice was supposed to be doing in London; the restaurant which Mr Benefer thought might see him through the autumn months. Even his mother, it turned out, could see the conveyor-belt of time slipping away. 'Nothing for you to do here,' she chided – they were having a late supper in the cottage with the light fading over the distant trees. 'Why don't you go and stay with your dad' – Alex's father lived in Leicester – 'where you could get a proper job and that?' It was the *and that* that sent the dart into the bull's eye – all the things Alex suspected were missing from his life and, if truth were to be known, he was glad to see gone. But it was Mr Benefer whose desires burned most brightly. There was no security in holiday shops; as he remarked, no one bought flip-flops and parasols in the winter months (Alex felt like saying that no one bought them from Mr Benefer at any time of the year.) 'That old fish place over by the green,' he explained to the captive audience of the counter. 'Taking a three-year lease. An all-the-year-round trade, you might say.' You might have said all kinds of things. 'All sorts of opportunities,' he added, which was as much a piece of bait as the tubs of maggots the anglers on the north shore laid out on the shingle next to their rods. 'Mr B as a *maitre d'*? I don't think so,' Marcus said. He was wearing a new pair of sunglasses that must have cost at least half his week's wages. 'I mean, how is he going to fit all the day's walks in?' Alex thought about it, and also about Hunstanton's pale autumn light, the silence that followed the passing of the last tourist and the wind coming in through the empty dunes.

On the afternoon following the morning on which Mr Benefer announced that he had signed the restaurant lease, would shortly be relinquishing the shop and called for volunteers to assist him in this exciting new adventure, they went down to the beach, officially to swim but really only to smoke and draw startling cross-hatched asteroids in the sand. It was then that the really dramatic thing happened, when a woman in an old-fashioned one-piece bathing-suit heading out to sea was taken unawares by an incoming wave and disappeared for several minutes, only to be brought out and resuscitated by a lifeguard. Alex, watching the woman's pale face, the lifeguard's hands busily at work and the gush of regurgitated sea-water, experienced a pang of existential dread, but Marcus took it in his stride. 'Mr B will be sorry to miss this,' Marcus said. 'His life could do with a little excitement. When we get back, I might give him some.'

There were no customers in the shop. Mr Benefer stood at the till, both hands pressed flat on the glass as if it threatened to rear up and overwhelm him. What remained of his hair needed cutting and grey strands sprang out in all directions. When he saw them he came out from behind the counter, moved into the space between them, extended both arms and clasped each of them by the shoulder. Close up he smelled of chicken fat.

'How are we doing boys?' he demanded.

'We're doing OK, Mr B,' Marcus said jauntily.

'And what are we going to do with ourselves this autumn?' he asked, with what in the circumstances was an excruciating archness.

'Mr B, I'll tell you,' Marcus said. Alex could tell that he was still amused by what was taking place, but only just. 'With all due respect, we're going to do exactly what we please.'

It was difficult to know exactly what happened in the next ten seconds or so. For an instant they hung together, suspended above the ground like the front row in a rugger scrum. Then there was a second or two in which Mr Benefer seemed to let go his grip on Alex and try to press Marcus more tightly to his side. Shortly after this Marcus said, 'Christ! Will you let go of my fucking arm?', and gave Mr Benefer a jab in the ribs that sent him crashing into a shelf full of Walker's crisps.

Outside on the esplanade – Marcus had been sacked on the spot, Alex seemed to have been let off with a caution – with the herring gulls swirling overhead, they went into a little huddle, like footballers talking tactics before a free-kick. Marcus, Alex could see, still had the light of battle in his eye. 'So,' he said, 'how are we doing?' Alex, knowing what this was about and remembering what Marcus had hinted about the flat in the Caledonian Road that was supposedly theirs for the asking, shook his head. 'It's OK,' Marcus said, still smiling at the memory of Mr Benefer hitting the crisp-stack. 'It's OK, Al. Never mind that lady on the beach. You're the one who's drowning in Hunny', the look on his face not quite contemptuous, or kindly, but something else, something else altogether, that hung tantalisingly in the air between them, like the scent of the cooking oil, the gulls sailing high on the thermals, framed by the bright blue sky and the dense, unruly sea.

Those Big Houses up Newmarket Road

I N THOSE DAYS, and in that part of Norwich – I am writing of a period more than forty years ago – social distinctions were a matter of crucial importance. In fact, it sometimes seemed that scarcely a day could go by without your having to calibrate or recalibrate a series of complex private codes – codes that were rendered that much more abstruse by virtue of their never being explicitly stated – with the aim of establishing what the people you rubbed up against in this late-teenage world were actually like. Sometimes this taxonomy was completely basic; at other times it was comparatively subtle – I am thinking of a woman my parents knew who was said to have 'bought a static caravan at Hemsby and made something of herself.' Sometimes it was narrowly concerned with status, as when somebody's father was introduced to the conversation as a Consultant at the Norfolk & Norwich Hospital, a Departmental Head at the Norwich Union Insurance Society or a Lecturer in Physics at the University of East Anglia, but even then there was no guarantee of precedence. My parents, for example, would have regarded the

insurance man as slightly less important than the consultant but much less significant than the science lecturer.
Other people would have thought differently.

Sometimes, on the other hand, the distinction was
geographical, and here even greater degrees of complexity
came into play. If everyone agreed that to come from West
Earlham, the bandit country of Larkman Lane and the
Bowthorpe Road, was social death, then there were other
parts of Norwich where spatial judgments were much less
easy to frame. My parents, again, were suspicious of people
who came from Thorpe – not because there was anything
wrong with this blameless suburb to the north of the city,
but because very few of their friends lived there. In much
the same way, at a classical concert at St Andrew's Hall,
my father once overheard a man whom he knew to reside
in Cringleford in south-west Norwich talking in what he
described as a 'lah-di-dah voice,' so that was Cringleford
gone. Then, naturally, there were behavioural, shading
into moral judgments, levelled at people who dressed in
ways of which other people did not approve, or whose social
antennae were not as finely attuned as they should have
been. Here, unusually, in a world built on plain-speaking,
which enjoyed calling a spade a spade, a certain amount of
irony prevailed. To particularise, 'She's rather nice, don't you
think?' meant its precise opposite. 'He has the gift of the
gab, don't you think?' practically guaranteed that whoever
was being spoken about was a vainglorious egomaniac.
Sometimes, alternatively, it was simply a case of pressing
any ammunition that was available into service, whether
it confirmed long-held opinions or blatantly contradicted
them. My father, again, approved of people with hearty

appetites; he disliked guests at his house who, as he put it, 'pingled their food.' But there were other kinds of virtue, mostly derived from sheer status, that could, on certain occasions, trump this drawback. I once saw my father entertain a Masonic friend of his, possibly even the master of his lodge, who spent forty minutes toying with a cheese salad, only to remark that 'he liked a man who didn't overindulge himself.'

I have mentioned all this, and at such length, because it seems the most appropriate backdrop to the story of my dealings, such as they were, with a girl called Lucy Fortescue. Appropriate, because they had nothing to do with romance, or interior myth-making, but were bound up in straightforward personal embarrassment. All this happened towards the end of 1977, and its roots lay in a conversation I had with a boy called James Mortimer, who in his way was another example of those finely-calibrated codes by which our adolescent world – other worlds, if it came to that – were governed. Which is to say that the people I knew called James – a popular boy's name in the late 1970s – were invariably referred to as 'Jimmy' or occasionally 'Jim.' There was nothing generational about this filing-down. Adults, parents, sometimes even headmasters, did it too. Even more to the point, most of the boys called James preferred the shortened version and would encourage you to call them by it. Sometimes this process of re-imagining went even further and an adjective would be tacked on, so that someone would spend four or five years being referred to as 'Tiny Jim' even when the boy in question, five foot two when the garnish was first applied, had grown into a hulking six-foot Leviathan. There was even a boy with a fractious temper who was known to the entire school as 'Mad Jimmy Parsons.' But for some reason, which I was never able to fathom, James Mortimer was always known as 'James Mortimer.' This ability to preserve the sanctity of his name was all the more remarkable in that he was completely innocuous. He had no charisma. He was not one of those boys who managed to get people to call them what they wanted to be called through sheer personal magnetism or force of will. He was not 'clever' – not always a point in your favour – or good at games or otherwise distinguished about the place. But still, he was always 'James Mortimer', whereas I, christened Francis, had been known as 'Franny' from the moment I first walked through the school gates.

But perhaps, on the other hand, it was merely that James – J. W. C. Mortimer major, to give him his full title – triumphed by dint of his sheer inoffensiveness, that all his virtues were negative ones. My parents, for example, professed to like him for characteristics that I never thought he possessed. He was 'not always showing off, like some of those friends of yours,' and his own parents lived modestly in a house on Unthank Road – standard upper-bourgeois accommodation, but not in any way drawing undue attention to itself. Again, I mention all this, and at such length, because the judgments it involved, and the materials from which they were constructed, seem to me to have some bearing on the story of Lucy Fortescue, although it should be pointed out that James Mortimer major played no part in it other than a catalytic one. What happened would probably not have happened, or not have happened in quite the same way, if he had kept his mouth shut. All the same, his role was only advisory and he was not in the least responsible for what ensued. In fact, the more I think about it, there was really no blame to be apportioned. Or if there was, it could simply be ascribed to the social forces that governed the world in which we moved, and were far too abstract and intangible to be brought to a court of law.

It was a Thursday afternoon towards the end of October, and having gone to great lengths to avoid playing rugby, James and I were sitting in the tea room of the Norwich Assembly House. We were talking, as we quite often talked, about girls, which is to say not about girls generally, or even the girls, known to us, who went to the Norwich High School and formed our female circle, but certain exclusive girls, not known to us, who went there. And here even more social distinctions instantly declared themselves. The Norwich High School for Girls was a fairly genteel establishment to begin with, but there existed on its strength girls who, socially, were quite out of the ordinary. They had names like Anastasia Featherstone-Coote, Diana Shaw-Stewart or Perdita Lestrange; they were the daughters of Air Vice-Marshals, Norfolk land-owners or Norwich Union executives; their mothers – one or two of them anyway – had been presented at court. None of which, naturally, meant that they had not been discriminated against in some way. The tradition among seriously rich people in Norfolk at this time was that sons went to boarding school while daughters had to make do with the Girls' Public Day School Trust. But Anastasia, Diana and Perdita – it was odd how many of these names ended in 'a' – and the others did not repine. They may have been hoopoes adrift on a lawn full of starlings, but the starlings were friendly, and in the manner of most passage migrants they knew they would soon be flying off else-where. And so James and I sat there talking about them in the way that boys of our class and temperament talked about girls in the late 1970s – familiarly and forensically, but also respectfully and wistfully, which is to say that had any of these girls arrived at the Assembly House, sat down at a table near us and so much as nodded in our direction we should have had no idea at all what to say to them.

And yet – something I should make plain at the outset – this was not a meeting of equals, for James – I was never quite sure how – knew more about the Anastasias and the Dianas and the Perditas than I did. He knew what schools their brothers went to, and he knew where they lived. Better even than this, he knew what their social lives consisted of, who they went around with, where they could be found. And so our conversations tended to consist of me, with an assumed diffidence, asking questions, and James, with a kind of offhand deliberation, answering them. They were intensely stylised conversations – they could hardly have been anything else – and they went like this:

'Marianne Ovenden?'

'The tall girl with the reddish hair? Off limits. Absolutely *verboten*.'

'Why's that exactly?'

'Saw her with Tony Clodd at the Inter-sixth social. And you know as well as I do that Tony Clodd could sprinkle you over his cornflakes and have you for breakfast.'

'Sally Fielden-Price?'

'Definite lesbian. No chance there.'

'Your evidence?'

'Saw her holding hands with Holly Leverson. I mean,

holding hands. Not just girlish chums out on a spree. White to the knuckle.'

'Amanda Jeavons?'

'Going off to New Zealand for a year as an *au pair*. You'd be wasting your time.'

'What about Lucy Fortescue?'

And here James hesitated. At the time I thought it was straightforward lack of information: the well had run dry; the gazetteer of schoolgirl talent had a missing page. Later I realised that I had misjudged him and his hesitation lay in the complexity of the data he had at his disposal, that Lucy Fortescue was not simply a pretty girl who might react favourably if you phoned her up; it was all much more complicated than that.

'Lucy Fortescue,' I said again, a bit alarmed by the silence.

'Yes?'

'You think I stand a chance?'

'You could go farther and fare worse.'

'Tell me what you know.'

'Lives in one of those big houses up Newmarket Road. Father's in London three days a week. Don't know what he does . . . Her mother's rather odd.'

'What do you mean, odd?'

'I don't know. Just *odd*.'

And there we were again, where we so often ended up in any discussion of what people were 'like', back in the realm of the unquantifiable. If all kinds of people in Norwich at this time could safely be described as 'odd', then, equally, oddity had its degrees, its tantalising grey areas, its quicksand stretches. T. J. C. Devereux minor, a teenage mathematician of something near genius, who collected bus tickets as a hobby, was 'odd'. My great aunt Iris, so terrified of the house burning down that she would pick up spent matches from the floor and hold them under the tap until they fell apart, was odd, and so was the elderly man who sat in Norwich Central Library writing poems with a clasp knife open beside him on the desk. How odd was Mrs Fortescue, whether run to ground in her big house in Newmarket Road or waylaid outside it? There was no way of telling. Here, as so often in teenage life, you were on your own.

As for what followed, the peculiarity is how little part in it was played by Lucy Fortescue herself. Except that she was on the short side, had an elfin look and, when you held it in yours, a remarkably sticky hand, I can remember hardly anything about her. Teenage relationships in those days, at any rate the teenage relationships in which people like James Mortimer and myself indulged, followed a predictable pattern. If the girl could be persuaded to go out with you – which wasn't always the case – you met her in the front entrance to Jarrold's department store and took her to a coffee shop. If everything went well, you might later escort her to a cinema. After about six weeks she would tell you – usually by letter, sometimes face to face – that it 'wasn't going anywhere' and return to her Cat Stevens albums or the collection of miniature porcelain animals with which she otherwise beguiled her leisure. The point I am making, I suppose, is that everything that happened in this particular relationship before it ended is purely incidental. It was only the final day that mattered – an occasion in which Lucy played only a supporting role and where her very presence was pretty much symbolic.

It was early December by this time, when the street lights started going on at 3.30 and not everybody, not even the most ardent swain, would necessarily agree to a suggestion that they 'might like to come round after school tomorrow.' But there I was, half an hour after the school had shut for the afternoon, making my way along St Stephen's, past the roundabout and towards Newmarket Road, one of the main arterial thoroughfares that led out of Norwich, and at this point filling up with traffic. Almost immediately, as I looked at the numbers on the house-gates, it became clear that James Mortimer's intelligence gathering had fallen short. The Fortescues did not live in one of the big houses on Newmarket Road; they lived in one of the biggest houses, almost at the far end and set back from the road, where substantial properties could be glimpsed through the trees of outsize gardens. In fact, 173, which took a good twenty minutes to find, looked as though it might be one of the biggest of all, a kind of mini-mansion with a turreted upper storey and what looked an orchard abutting its right hand side. There was something Gothic about it, not so much about the house itself as the setting: the long gravel drive, the massed trees and of course the darkness, which even ten yards from the road was pretty much impenetrable. The branches of the apple trees hung low and spectral; there were small animals scuffling in the undergrowth. But still I pressed on, school briefcase in one hand, Robin's Records bag in which lay a copy of Fleetwood Mac's *Rumours* in the other, conscious that I was in uncharted territory, that I had absolutely no idea what to expect, that anything, or more likely nothing, could happen.

The gravel drive eventually fetched up in an ellipse of raised paving stones and a studded front door, about eight feet high, which resembled the entrance point to a medieval castle. Several moments passed before Lucy, still in her school uniform and holding a cup of tea in one hand, tugged it open.

'You'd better come in,' she said.

'It's nice to see you.'

'Yes it is,' she said, not quite despairingly but with a kind of uncertainty that made me suspect that something was up, that some gigantic piece of scenery had swung into place that threatened to dwarf the two actors who stood on the stage in front of it and which they could do nothing about.

'Did you have a good day at school?' We were standing in the hallway by now, and I was hanging up my coat – an all-encompassing Canadian RAF greatcoat bought at the Army Surplus shop, which was against school rules – on a coat-hook in the shape of a stag's antler.

'I had a day at school. Have you had your hair cut? It looks funny.'

I had had my hair cut, but it did not look funny – or at any rate no funnier than anyone else's.

'We'll go in here,' she said.

To the left of the vestibule, which was about the same size as the entire ground floor of my parents' house a mile away on Christchurch Road, there was an ante-room full of austere-looking furniture and a piano – what my father's generation would have called a parlour. At first sight the woman who got up from the chair she had been sitting in looked like a fair proportion of the middle-aged women you saw in Norwich at this time – of medium height, thin-lipped and with a permed hair-do that a Force Ten gale would probably not have disturbed. It was only when she loomed into view that you realised that all the character-istics of the middle-class Norwich housewife had been slightly exaggerated, that the lips were even thinner, the face paler and the hair marcelled up to the point of parody. As this apparition heaved into sight, Lucy said: 'This is my mother. Mummy, this is Francis.'

'*Linda* Fortescue,' Mrs Fortescue said, but in a tone that suggested the back garden was piled high with the mummified corpses of young men who had made the mistake of calling her by her Christian name.

'Delighted to meet you, Mrs Fortescue.'

I was used to girls' mothers being tough nuts to crack. It was what they did, how they behaved, what they were there for. They sat on their sofas and glared and it was up to you to correct all the misconceptions that had followed you in through the front door. On the other hand, Mrs Fortescue – Linda – was clearly in a class of her own. As well as the dead white face and the over-applied lipstick, which made her look like a piece of veal on the butcher's block, she had popping blue eyes so pronounced that they seemed to give off sparkles with each darting glance.

'I suppose you're one of Lucy's young men.'

'Oh, don't be silly Mummy,' Lucy said glumly, but Mrs Fortescue breezed on regardless.

'I always wonder exactly what that means these days. Do you go and hold hands in the park? I should have thought it was rather cold for that at this time of year.'

I was starting to take in my surroundings by this time, or enough of them to see that the parlour wall displayed several portraits of evil-looking old men and some pictures of horses by Sir Alfred Munnings, while the Regency wallpaper would have made a suitable backdrop for the Bennet sisters as they sat playing whist of an evening. Like Mrs Fortescue, the room bore certain resemblances to other homes I had visited while having got completely out of hand. What on earth would she say next, I wondered, and what would I say in return? In fact, her next sally was far more conventional, so much so as to be faintly disappointing.

'So, what are you going to do with yourself?' she demanded.

I could deal with this. It was what practically every adult you met in a social situation asked you, and it referred to your plans for higher education.

'I'm thinking of going to Oxford,' I said.

'My husband was at Cambridge,' Mrs Fortescue countered, not however failing to disguise a very faint flicker of interest. 'Which college?'

I told her. 'That's one of the smaller ones, isn't it?' she wondered. 'I daresay you'll spend all your time taking the warden's dog for walks. If you get in, that is.'

Now and again during these exchanges, I found myself looking at Lucy – not exactly to see if she would offer any support, but just to establish how she was taking it – and her face was quite impassive. It was how her mother behaved, and you put up with it, like a tax demand or a diagnosis of impetigo.

'In any case,' Mrs Fortescue said decisively, 'I think people make far too much of a fuss about university these days, especially for girls. There are lots of other things to do.' Lucy, who I knew wanted to study Law at Durham, stirred gloomily. Now, all this, even allowing for the scent of exaggeration, was par for the course. It was what a certain type of woman said in the presence of anyone who was showing an interest in their daughter, and it was not meant to be personal. But what Mrs Fortescue said next lifted her out of the lane of mild eccentricity and placed her squarely in the channel of border-line insanity.

'*What is that bag?*'

For a moment I thought she had her eye on my school briefcase, a really smart affair with my initials in gilt capitals under the handle. But no, she meant the bag with the Fleetwood Mac album in it.

'What are Robin's Records?'

It should be said that at this point in time anyone who walked round Norwich for more than a few minutes would have seen at least half-a-dozen Robin's Records bags. They were what teenagers carried their record collections around in, prior to swapping them in the school playground.

'It's a record shop. In Pottergate.'

'*A record shop?*' Mrs Fortescue said, as if this was some nefarious sexual practice, mention of which had outraged the sanctity of her home. 'I don't think I have been in a record shop in my life.'

'Oh, don't be silly Mummy,' Lucy said again, even more glumly than before. 'You went into one to buy the *Sound of Music* album that time.'

It was about twenty past five. There was no knowing

how long this interrogation would go on. My tea would be waiting at home. Mrs Fortescue seemed to sense this discomfort and said something even more outlandish.

'You young people have such odd hobbies these days . . . Let's have a game of snap.'

At any subsequent period in my life – even a month or two later – this would have been the moment to leave. But I was a well-brought-up middle-class boy who had drunk in the obligation to defer to adults, to indulge their whims and conciliate their idiosyncrasies, with my mother's milk. If Mrs Fortescue had suggested that she put on an exhibition of Scottish country dancing or read Kierkegaard aloud in the original Danish, I am pretty sure I should have agreed. The snap cards came in an ancient, greasy packet. The cards were of fancifully-drawn animals: roguish hippos; three-toed sloths; zebras with chunky, oblong teeth. We sat down in a little huddle at the end of the table and began to play. For a while nothing much happened, although Mrs Fortescue seemed to be concentrating very hard. Lucy, whose face was absolutely blank, spotted a pair of rhinoceri and claimed them. Then Lucy and her mother each produced a highly anthropomorphised orang-utan.

'Snap!' I said.

'Snap!' Mrs Fortescue hissed, a millisecond later, and picked up the cards.

I was so startled by this, so thoroughly flummoxed, that I simply sat and gaped. Nothing happened for a moment or so until Lucy carried off a pair of giraffes. Then I played what might have been an ibex and Mrs Fortescue followed with its duplicate.

'Snap!' I said.

'Snap!' Mr Fortescue echoed, and then, as if there were a faint scintilla of doubt that needed clarifying, 'Mine, I think.'

Even then, I showed no sign of the annoyance I felt. That was not how you behaved in those days, not to a middle-aged woman in the parlour of whose big house you were sitting in. Instead I got to my feet, put the remainder of my cards down on the table and said:

'I'm really sorry, but I shall have to be going.'

'Must you?' demanded Mrs Fortescue, with what seemed genuine disappointment. 'Must you really? I was rather enjoying myself.'

'Yes I must,' I said. 'But thank you.;

And that, more or less, was that. If Lucy said anything as I made my way to the door I don't remember it. In any case, I knew it was all over between us and that we would never exchange another word, that whatever happened I could never regard her in the way I had regarded her before. The door closed behind me and I started off over the ellipse of paving stones, breathing heavily and, I discovered, trembling with rage. It was about twenty to six, and the tea, which my mother always put out, whether I was there to eat it or not, would be growing cold. There was fine rain falling, and in the distance the lights of a dense rectangular shape moving behind the tree-cover showed that a bus was going by. All this – Mrs Fortescue's popping blue eyes, the game of snap, the evil old men staring out of their frames – made me suddenly resolute. When I grew up, I thought, I would find a way of buying one of those big houses in Newmarket Road. Whether this would be a stab at solidarity or an act of revenge remained to be seen. The rain was coming down harder now, and the Robin's Records bag banged against my calf. And so I set off, back down the drive and into the road beyond, where mouldering horse-chestnut trees quivered in the breeze and concertina'd traffic hung bumper to bumper, deep into the heart of a yet unfallen world.

Special Needs

THE BAYFIELDS – Emmagem and Carrie – lived in a Housing Association property on the new estate at Brundall. As ever, the social housing came squeezed in at the end of the rows, with porthole windows and two shiny front-doors side by side to spare general embarrassment, but to Emmagem, who had once lived in an actual slum in Mountergate before the bulldozers rolled in, the whole thing was a paradise on earth. Sometimes they went into Norwich to shop, but the buses were unreliable and Carrie was unnerved by the big wide pavements and the crowded coffee parlours, so mostly they stayed at home and lived out of convenience stores. There were fixed rules as to what Carrie was permitted to cook. She was allowed to boil soup or put pizza in the oven if Emmagem was in the next room, but mainly she helped out, arranged chips neatly on metal trays and stared out of the window at the diggers on the edge of the estate as they tore up tree-roots to make way for the next sprawl of housing.

Carrie was a big, untidy girl with permanently disarranged hair who nobody had ever been able to do anything about. When she was younger and they were living in Lakenham, the authorities had despatched her to a special school where she glued pieces of felt onto cardboard triangles and sang songs about Hector the Mountain Goat. After that there had been talk of teaching her to use a sewing-machine and crochet ornamental place-mats, but Emmagem, knowing it wouldn't work, declined these overtures. Nobody seemed to mind. Now and again people rang up from the social services and suggested day-care centres and therapeutic residential weekends, but these too were resisted. Day-care centres and therapeutic residential weekends meant noise and bustle and packed rooms and eager women with clipboards, all of which Carrie abhorred. And so they hunkered down in Brundall, going for walks and patronising the fast-food joints and the hen cabins, with occasional visits to Carrie's nan, who, never quite taking in the situation, always said that Carrie was a big girl and had she got a boyfriend, with £200 hoarded in an old pickle jar against emergencies. Night-times, when the wind blew in over the exposed plain created by the torn-down trees, they sat before the gas-fire and watched *Emmerdale, Brookside, Coronation Street, East Enders, Love Island* and *Celebrity Big Brother,* mingling the soaps and the reality shows so indiscriminatingly that the characters seemed to glide from life to its spangled approximation from one moment to the next.

But there were always things to think about here in Brundall, with the rain scudding in against the roof, the car-doors slamming in the street and the kids rushing blithely home from school. One of them, naturally, was Carrie, who at thirty had turned sulky and less biddable, sometimes yelled at the TV and had to be calmed down

with cups of sugar-sweetened cocoa or – occasionally –
vodka shots. Another was time itself which, when they
lived in Lakenham, had drifted by, but now seemed to
race past with astonishing speed. A third, and undoubtedly
the equal of the preceding two, was Neil. Neil, met at
a car-boot held on the playing fields of the local second-
ary school, was, Emmagem had to concede, the kind of
man you met at car-boots: thin, bunchy, unattached, yet
harbouring welcome depths of expertise. The car-boot
blokes all had knacks. They could do electrical repairs,
or concoct home-brewed beer, or mend furniture. Neil's
knack was narrowly domestic. He put saucers full of water
on the bricks in front of the gas-fire to keep the air cool
and fixed the mould in the shower-room by hammering
in a ventilator duct. Even better, he knew what to do when
Carrie kicked off, removed sharp objects that might cause
difficulty, interposed himself between Carrie's flailing
limbs and items of furniture and made them all cups of
tea when it was over.

'Where you from then?' Emmagem had asked that first
time in the pub, back from the car-boot with a scratched
vinyl copy of *Carpenters' Greatest Hits* in her tote-bag, and
Neil had murmured something about working on the rigs,
driving jobs, a stint in London that had plunged him into
(unspecified) jeopardy. This, too, was characteristic of the
car-boot men. Vague about paid employment, careers and
track-records, they were even vaguer about wives, children
and emotional attachments. In the end Emmagem established that there was a Mrs Neil living in Toftwood on the
other side of Dereham and a court-case (again unspecified)
pending. Still, there were things to be said in Neil's favour.

There was the reliable way in which he turned up when he said he would and left when he said he would; there was the battered Škoda in which buzzed them all down the Acle Straight to Great Yarmouth one summer afternoon; there was the undoubted fact that Carrie liked him; and there was his tact when it came to her behaviour, habits and temperament. One or two previous Neils had said blunt things about Carrie and been told where they could shove it. Emmagem, watching her trailing him round the house and demanding 'Where Neil?' whenever he stepped outside for a smoke – he was good about that, too – was alternately charmed and worried by what this unique set of circumstances might portend.

'Gets his feet under the table, Neil do,' one of the car-boot men had said in a friendly way when all this went semi-public, and Emmagem had smiled, nodded and filed the warning away for future reference, together with her discovery that the pickle-jar tally had sunk to £120. They took to going out in the Škoda on Sundays, to Blofield Heath, Sheringham Park, destinations even further afield. Carrie liked the rhododendrons in the park, which were monstrous things, twice the size of any flowering shrub Emmagem had ever set eyes on, and said 'What that Neil?' whenever the next riot of colour loomed into view. Rhododendron bushes; Double Magnum choc-ices from the convenience store deep-freeze; Neil's parched face: that was how Emmagem recalled the summer that followed. There were problems with the sleeping arrangements, what with Carrie barging in at 3 a.m. in search of mislaid cuddly toys, but they got by. In the morning they watched Neil do his press-ups – fifty or sixty at a time, eyes out on stalks, with a quick hand-clap to mark their passage – in front of the blaring TV, while Carrie boiled milk – another thing she was allowed to do – for the porridge and weak summer sun made shadow-patterns on the carpet.

The advice, when it started coming in, was thoroughly innocuous. 'Ever get anyone to look at her?' Neil wondered one evening when they were sitting by the tiny square of abandoned back lawn watching Carrie hunt for tennis balls in the overgrown grass. 'She's all right,' Emmagem said, which did not mean Carrie was all right but that it was no one's business but hers. That night when Neil tried her with *The Tale of the Flopsy Bunnies* Emmagem left them to it. This kind of thing had happened before. Neil's sister's friend Angie, who lived nearby and had experience of paediatric nursing, was quietly rebuffed. 'Where Neil?' Carrie demanded while Neil was driving her back to Hemblington. They'd had soup the previous night, but Emmagem produced a couple of tins of oxtail as a diversionary tactic. Two days after that, when Carrie went spectacularly tonto, fell over the portable heater and gashed her head on the side of a radiator, Neil was providentially on hand to drive them to the Norfolk & Norwich. Looking at him as they made their way down the A47, with her hand pressing the wad of tissues against Carrie's bloodied scalp – Carrie went into semi-shock on these occasions and made mournful chirruping noises – Emmagem could see the glint of stern resolve in his eyes, a steely yet well-nigh theatrical determination to play his part in the drama unfolding around them.

The nurses at A&E knew Emmagem of old. 'All right love?' one of them said. 'Doing OK darlin'' Emmagem returned 'How's yourself?' It was swiftly established that, while Carrie had not fractured her skull, stitches would be required, and so they waited for a couple of hours – it was Saturday night and the place was full of drunks – to be seen. Neil fetched plastic cups of pallid coffee from the machine, went out to feed pound coins into the meter ('Where Neil?' Carrie asked, drowsily), menaced one of the drunks when he strayed too close and juggled the furry tiger that had come with them to her great delight. By 2 a.m., when the nurse came to collect her, they were all snuggled together, half-asleep, with the tiger crammed flat between Carrie and Neil's inclined heads. Thanking him afterwards, out in the airy, pre-dawn car-park, with the stitches bulging out of the square inch or so of Carrie's scalp they'd had to shave, Emmagem knew she meant it.

And of course the stake-out at A&E changed something. These things always did. Hadn't Emmagem married Carrie's dad mostly because he'd smacked his car into a tree with her in the passenger seat beside him? 'There's things that girl could do,' Neil said once or twice, not exactly reproachfully but halfway near it. 'Oh yeah, what things?' Emmagem wanted to know. 'Classes she could go to,' Neil said. Emmagem, transfixed by the vision of Carrie, white-faced and quivering, in the back row of the last such class she had attended, shook her head. Just lately Neil had taken to combing out Carrie's hair of an evening. The brisk, decisive strokes made it seem longer than it really was and had the effect of emphasizing the chunky contours of Carrie's face. 'Could be – what's her name? – Janis Joplin,' Neil said, and Emmagem, despite not knowing whether she approved or not, knew what he meant.

Matters came to a head in the kitchen one autumn night, with a handful of leaves from the few trees left behind by the diggers caught in the corners of the window-frames and over-bright light bouncing off the surfaces: Carrie boiling soup; Emmagem and Neil by the fridge. 'That's good soup lovey,' Neil said – he had taken to calling her 'lovey.' 'I can smell how good it is. You see,' he explained to Emmagem, as if Carrie weren't in the room, 'she needs encouraging. You encourage her and she'll do more.' 'Encourage her to do what?' Emmagem said. 'What's she supposed to do?' She was annoyed at Neil, who seemed to think he could wave some magic wand and have Carrie executing a *pas seul* or scrapping with the MMA harpies. 'Music and movement,' Neil said, in his patient, whiny way. 'You could get her to do that.' Emmagem thought about the music and movement classes and the bright, birdlike girls who conducted them, and the shame that would follow from Carrie's exposure to them. 'Why don't you fuck off?' she said. 'No, I mean it. Why don't you *fuck off*?' 'Don't you tell me to fuck off,' Neil said, who had a truculent side, and Carrie, catching the tang of discontent, turned to face them, ladle in hand. 'Don't you be nasty to my mum,' she said. 'That's all right lovey,' Neil said. 'No one's being nasty to anyone. You just make your nice soup.' But there was something in this that irked Carrie even more. 'Don't you be nasty,' she said, hand tightening on the pan. 'Listen lovey,' Neil said. 'When we've had our soup I'll brush your hair out for you, OK? Brush your hair and make you look nice.' But it was no good, and with a dexterity of which Emmagem had previously thought her incapable, Carrie threw the pan at him. The soup, though not quite at boiling point, was still hot enough to do damage. And Emmagem, watching the steam rising off Neil's agonised forehead and Carrie's white knuckles raised to her chin, felt for all the world like some bygone tightrope walker, buffeted by the wind, teetering on her span above the angry river, who against all the odds has managed to regain her balance.

In the Land of Grey and Pink

S IX MONTHS INTO what Jasmine's mum still called 'the new arrangements', a certain kind of routine had begun to impose itself. To begin with, there was the breakfast in the grim Bowthorpe dawn: the heaped bowl of Sugar Puffs for Jas; some fancy pile of muesli or other that looked as if it was made of twigs and baler twine for Carmella; with little Bradley, outsize pacifier jammed into his mouth, staring wide-eyed from the stroller. Then there was the goading of Carm's decades-old hatchback out into the dense thoroughfare of Larkman Lane, up into Marlpit to deliver little Bradley to the childminder (Emmalyne was a good sort and didn't mind these 7 a.m. drop-offs.) After that came the agitated drive through snarled traffic along the main road into Norwich, with its incidental scene-swellers: the big municipal trucks upending garbage bins outside the KFC cabins and the burger bars; the commuter taxis ploughing in along the empty bus-lanes; the party people loitering back to student bed-sitters or stopping off to sprawl on benches in the park. And then, twenty or thirty minutes later, there was the stashing of the car, usually in the side-street up the far end of Pottergate where no warden was ever known to venture, but sometimes in Barry's mate Nigel's rank-smelling lock-up, followed by the breathless scuttle – neither Jasmine nor her mum were terribly good at walking – through the snaggle of bunched alleyways, over the road beyond the Guildhall and down past the war memorial to the marketplace.

Here, under a grey sky going pink at the edges, another kind of routine kicked in: less scenic but more concentrated. First, taking care not to bang your feet and listening out for the ping of Ashley's uniformly irritating texts, you started taking down the heavy wooden shutters and piling them up at the back of the stall. Then you up-ended the tenner's worth of small change that constituted the float into the unlocked till and checked to see if the card machine, which as Carm had often remarked, had a mind of its fucking own, was still working, and if it wasn't you taped a hand-written sign on the till which said CASH SALES ONLY. After that you shifted the stock around a bit in what you hoped was an advantageous manner and retrieved the stash of sales cards, advertising flyers and three-for-two promotional bannerets from under the counter. After that, by which time the City Hall clock, if it was working, would be chiming eight, you could allow yourself a break – go off round the pitches at the lower end, say, nod to the shouty bloke who sold replica football kits and the boys on the fish stall or fetch a coffee from the takeaway bar on the far side near the taxi-rank, and smoke your third cigarette of the morning – the first one had been smoked in the car and the second one in the scamper up from the parking-lot. After that – after all that – it was time to sit grandly behind your till, puffa jacket buttoned up under your chin against the cold, vigilant and alert, waiting for the customers, the customers who would surely come.

On mornings when the customers did not come – this happened quite a lot – you sat and talked. Sometimes you talked about little Bradley, and how when you hadn't been there the other night to put him to bed he had stared fixedly and inconsolably at the gaping space which you should have filled. Sometimes you talked about the denizens of whichever West Earlham hostelry Carm had spent the previous evening in and their exploits towards closing time ('Nah, I mean it was *really fucking quiet* for once.') This particular morning, on the other hand, found you talking about that vital part of the day's endeavours, the merchandise.

'Mum, we're going to have to stop stocking those mirrors.'

'Why? What's wrong with them?'

'Out of date, aren't they? I mean, nobody's going to buy a mirror with Robbie Williams on it. Not these days. Not now. Or that Ginger Spice either.'

'So who do they want on them then?'

Just at that moment Jasmine's phone pinged. It was one of Ashley's plaintive ones. *How is little feller?* She gave it a second or two and texted back *Like you fucking care, tosser.*

'I don't know. Ariane Grande, Dua Lipa. Taylor Swift.'

'Is that that one that sang at the Superbowl?' Carmella had never really kept up with popular culture. She was still impressionably at large in a world of Spice Girls, Backstreet Boys and Katie and Pete. *Cd cum n see him 2nite* Ashley texted back. *In yr dreams*, Jasmine returned. As well as the celebrity mirrors, the stall sold fruit-flavoured vapes, novelty key-rings, phone covers and watch-straps.

'All I'm saying is that it wouldn't hurt to try some different lines. Send some of the old stuff back and get some new stuff in.'

'Alfie at the depot won't like that.' The stock came from a rambling warehouse on the outskirts of Peterborough otherwise filled with knock-off jeans and discontinued lines of Airwear.

'Alfie can lump it. I'll ring him now if you want,' Jasmine volunteered, suddenly feeling like one of those hotshot businesswomen you saw in TV dramas, dressed in sober black two-pieces with an exotic cocktail to hand and not taking any shit.

It was getting on for 8.30 now, which was the market's first busy time. A man on his way to work bought a plastic wallet. Down at the fruit and veg stall a group of international students from the university were queuing up to purchase kumquats and packets of dates. There were times – these times usually, a couple of hours into what was clearly going to be a long and exhausting day – when Jasmine wondered about Carmilla. Basically Jasmine liked her mum, who had been very good about little Bradley and the domestic crises that had preceded his arrival. On the other hand, she wasn't always what you could call reliable, and the fact that she knew Ashley's mum and was therefore a ready audience for all kinds of stealthy propagandising on loser-boy's behalf, made this unreliability even worse. In fact, there were times – and this was one of them – when, examining her mother's creased but still narrowly juvenile face as it bobbed up and down alongside her at the till, Jasmine wondered just exactly what the fuck was going on, and what Carmilla thought she was up to, and that 45 was a bit old for Michelin Woman-style shell-suits and bubble perms and late evenings in mixed company at the Fiveways tavern. But then it did not do to condemn others because, however unwittingly, you could end up condemning yourself, and remembering that for all your good intentions and fixity of purpose you'd ended up with little Bradley and this terrible job and Ashley sending you whiny texts from whichever Costessey slapper's bedroom he'd happened to fetch up in that morning.

'You handle it then,' said Carmilla, with an unexpected moroseness, and they looked at each other with that pitiless mother-and-daughter candour that even now was capable of knocking Jasmine back on her heels. There were girls Jasmine knew whose mums doted on them, who brought them breakfast in bed, renewed their eyeliner stocks and drove away potential boyfriends on the grounds that no one could ever be good enough for their little Kylie or Adriana. On the other hand, you could do worse than a gone-to-seed 45 year-old with a schoolgirl's face, nicotine-ravaged fingers and no known vices – unless you counted Barry – beyond a half-pound-a-day wine gum habit.

And so the morning passed. The Robbie Williams mirrors lay rusting in their frames, the card machine packed up again and the Socialist Workers set up a stall outside the bank protesting about the invasion of Palestine. Big Connor, who worked for his dad at the clothing stall two rows up, came lumbering by and Carmilla and Jasmine went through their usual routine, which was for Carm to murmur 'Fancies the arse off you, that one,' and Jas – about thirty per cent flattered to seventy per cent outraged – languidly reply 'Give over, mum.' It was warmer now, but the sky was still gunmetal grey. 'Why don't you go and have your break?' Carmilla said at 12.15, turning unexpectedly solicitous, and she found herself walking down Gentleman's Walk, where a Jewish man in a skullcap was shouting things at the Socialist Workers, and on to the Back of the Inns, where, as well as the café where she bought her Cornish pasty, there was the added attraction of her friend Louisa.

Inside the shop, almost lost amid the fern fronds and the spreading artificial verdure, Louisa was assuring one of her customers that she intended to harmonise every single colour in the former's palette if it killed her. Jasmine waited humbly in the doorway until this apparition, who was carrying an actual fucking Lacoste bag, strode out into the street and then drifted hesitantly into view.

'Haven't seen you for a while,' Louisa acknowledged, dialling down the tones in which she had addressed Mrs Lacoste to something approximating normal conversational usage.

And no more she hadn't, Jasmine privately conceded, and for reasons that were best not gone into. 'Bit busy,' she said. There were, as she also privately conceded, problems about her visits to Louisa's shop. One of them was her unfeigned admiration for Louisa, who, while only in her late twenties, had not only managed to start her own interior design business but could talk posh when she wanted to and make it seem the most natural thing in the world.

'That stall,' Louisa said judiciously and with emphasis, '*that stall* will be the death of you. How's Bradley?'

'He's good. Eating his yoghurt now. And those rusks.'
For once Jasmine did not want to talk about little Bradley.
She wanted to talk about the bright, purposeful world of
interior design, which had captured her heart ever since,
at the impressionable age of fourteen, she had first accompanied Carm on one of her cleaning jobs at a newly-refur-
bished house in Cringleford. Just then the mobile on the
desk rang and she listened, mesmerised, as Louisa touched
up her accent again and told the person at the other end
that whatever she wanted done to her gazebo would doubt-
less cost 'another three or four K, tops.'

'What you want,' Louisa said, having dropped one or
two other tantalising phrases like 'gilt and gold surround'
and 'might work with taupe' into the mix and then ended
the call with the words 'Ciao for now', 'is some work experience.' Outside there were lunch-time shoppers hurtling
by and the clack of their heels resounded on the pavement.
'We're doing up this place in Taverham. Want to come and
have a go? Or would it interfere with your arrangements?'

Jasmine thought about the logistical nightmare that
this would entail: little Bradley; her mum having to work
the stall in solitude; all the rest of it. 'I'll sort something
out,' she said.

'You do that,' Louisa said complicitly, beckoning her
into a world of shared secrets and all-girl camaraderie.
'Take care of yourself.'

Back on Gentleman's Walk, where the Socialist Workers
were being moved on by a pair of haughty policewomen,
and emboldened by the memory of the phantasmal jungle
from which she had just emerged and the pasteboard business card Louisa had pressed into her hand which said

Louisa M. Gudgin & Associates, Design and Decoration, Jasmine took out her mobile and decided not only to phone Alfie at the depot in Peterborough but to take a firm line with him while she was about it.

'That you, Jas? 'Ow's your mum?'

'She's OK.' Alfie always sounded as if he was marooned on some perilously exposed crag with the winds whistling around his ears. 'You know them mirrors we got?'

'Robbie Williams in his majesty? Celine Dion, music's carnival queen?' Alfie had a whimsical side. 'What about them?'

'They don't sell shit. Need something more up-to-date. Taylor Swift and stuff. You can have the others back.'

'Hang on. Hang on. You want to send stuff *back*?' There were sea gulls flapping round the exposed crag now, wanting to peck at Alfie's hair. 'Fuck's sake, Jas. No returns or exchanges. Says in the small print.'

'Never seen no small print.'

'Well, take it from me it's there,' Alfie said, sounding a bit less strident. 'Can have the Taylor Swifts for £100 a dozen.'

'Look Alfie, you send me a couple of dozen of the Taylor Swifts and then I won't ask where all those Wrangler jeans we saw last time we was there came from.'

'Jesus, Jas.'

'Fucking knock-offs those jeans are. You could get done for that.'

'Taylor Swift,' Alfie said, reverting to whimsy. 'America's sweetheart. Her Superbowl *chanteuse*. All right darlin'?' The phantom wind whistled round his head again and he was gone.

All this was very satisfying. Slightly less agreeable was meeting Connor on the way back to the stall, big Connor, who must have weighed fifteen stone and whom she had once seen eat four Big Macs one after another with evident relish. It was the usual kind of thing. 'All right, Jas?' 'Fuck's sake, Connor.' 'You want to come and have a burger?' 'Fuck's sake, Connor.' 'Your mum OK?' 'Fuck's *sake*.' Less satisfactory even than this was coming back to the stall and finding Carm with that blissed-out look on her face and another cigarette a-dangle from her fingers, which meant that Bastard Barry was somewhere in the vicinity.

'Sell anything then?' Jasmine wanted to know.

'Couple of vapes. Bloke bought a key-ring and one of them football scarves.'

'Blind bloke, was he?'

Like the celebrity mirrors, the football scarves had not been a good idea. For a start, they were so short you could barely wind them twice round your neck. Worse, none of the players depicted on them looked at all like their originals. Thus Cristiano Ronaldo had the face of an anguished pig, while Harry Kane was clearly masquerading as an exhausted vampire back from a long night's haunting.

'Said he was buying it for his kid . . . Hello stranger' – this to Barry, who came sidling round the corner of the stall with a well-packed carrier bag in one hand and the usual perplexed expression on his big, seamed face.

'Ladies,' Barry said, giving them one of his patented gap-toothed grins and slamming the carrier bag down on the counter so that two bags of crisps and a Twix bar spilled out onto the glass. Staring at him as he stood blinking at

Carmilla, Jasmine found the look of tolerant disdain with which she usually regarded her mother's boyfriends turning just a little less tolerant and just a little more disdainful. Barry, it had to be conceded, was not exactly love's young dream. He was a big, top-heavy, clueless fifty-something, good-natured (mostly) but with an irascible side, who worked, or purported to work as a security guard in the Castle shopping mall. Jasmine, ranking him against the other blokes with whose affections her mother had toyed in the past decade and a half, had been forced to admit that he was a man of extremes: certainly the fattest; possibly the stupidest; definitely the least practical. Carm, it had to be said, adored him and got cross – *fucking* cross – if you tried to do him down.

'What you been up to then?' she now enquired. 'What you been doing with yourself?'

'Getting some food in,' Barry gravely disclosed. 'Chips. Couple of saveloys. You girls care to join me?'

Jasmine left the lovebirds to it and wandered out into the space between the two furthermost rows of stalls, which served as a thoroughfare between the Walk, City Hall and the buildings beyond it. Here there were people buying pairs of trousers and a smell of fish, and there were lunch-time drinkers standing in the doorway of the Sir Garnet Wolseley, beer glasses raised to the level of their chests. She walked up and down for a while, thinking about little Bradley and the big house at Taverham, and Barry and Carm, whom instinct told her were up to something. Sure enough, when she got back to the stall Fat Boy had upped and gone, leaving only a chip-wrapper and an atomised crisp or two to mark his passing, and Carm had one of those calculating but slightly storm-crossed looks on her face that spelled trouble.

'He's all right isn't he, Barry?'

Jasmine had passed this way before. 'He's a loser, mum.'

Carm ignored this. 'What would you say if I said I'd told him he could move in?'

Jasmine had passed this way before as well, and knew that the trick was to deflect. 'Where's he living now?'

'Some place up Dereham Road with a couple of mates . . . It's not ideal,' Carmilla allowed.

'How much is he going to pay?'

'Forty . . . fifty. He won't be no trouble,' Carm said valiantly. 'Thinks the world of little Bradley.'

'When's he ever seen little Bradley?' Jasmine wondered whether to introduce the subject of the Taverham work experience and decided to keep quiet about it for the moment. You needed trump cards in your dealings with Carm, and this was a wowser. The thought of the big house and the smell of fresh paint and the peacock's fan of Louisa's colour cards – all the seductive protocols of interior decoration – went racketing through her head again and she abandoned what she was going to say about Barry eating like a sodding horse and not to take less than sixty and smiled in what she hoped was an encouraging way.

'You're a good girl, Jas,' Carmilla said, without much conviction, and the two women examined each other in that way they had – not quite rancorous and not quite affectionate – as the sea gulls skirmished in the wide sky and somebody dropped a beer glass outside the Sir Garnet Wolseley and the band of buskers outside Lloyds Bank started up on 'Get Back', which, together with 'All Right

Now' and 'Message in a Bottle,' was one of the three songs
they knew.

◊

And so here they were a fortnight later, ten days after the
new stock had arrived, a week after Barry had moved in,
forty-eight hours after the day's work experience at the
big house in Taverham. And how had that gone, Jasmine
asked herself, stretching up to unhook the topmost shutter and tweaking a muscle just under her rib-cage, before
dealing with a text from Ashley that went *u want get tgethr
4 drink hun?* with the words *no fucking way*, how had that
worked out? Miraculously, the new stock had gone down
well and the takings were £100 a week up. Even better,
Carm had been impressed and Alfie, noting the increased
volume of traffic, had agreed to let them have another lot
at a 10 per cent discount. As for Barry's introduction to
the Bowthorpe flat, together with three suitcases and such
improbable items as a sun-lamp, a bag of golf-clubs and
seven miniature koi carp in a portable aquarium, its most
obvious consequence was a whole new set of routines to
add to the ones that already existed: Barry incinerating
bits of bread in the oven on the grounds that 'them toasters
never do the job'; Melanie, Barry's ex, ringing up at all
hours of the night; Barry's outsize torso hunched over the
steering wheel as he drove them in in the morning. A trail
of his baggage – real and metaphorical – lay around the
flat waiting to confound you at a second's notice: Barry's
scratch-cards; Barry's lottery tickets; Barry's weird tobacco,
which looked like powdered horse dung; Barry's carrier

bags, full of startlingly miscellaneous junk – all these had begun to make their presence felt on tables, chairs, carpets and kitchen floats. If there was a consolation it lay in the big house at Taverham, at which Jasmine had spent an idyllic day stripping the render off the kitchen wall and prepping the dining room ceiling for its first undercoat. 'What you want to do that for?' Carmilla had enquired – suspiciously – when the scheme was first unveiled to her. 'It's work experience, mum. Louisa said she'd give me a trial.' 'Is that that posh girl up Swan Lane?' 'She's not posh, mum. She used to live on the Tuckswood estate.' 'Yeah, like Princess fucking Di,' Carmilla said, and left it at that.

And now, Jasmine had to concede, there was something else going on in her life to add to the distractions of the big house at Taverham, the nightly spectacle of Barry feeding his miniature koi carp with pinches of fish food, the new stock and the sight of little Bradley, if not exactly taking his first steps, then hauling himself up the side of his stroller and venturing a half-stride or two. This was her acceptance, two afternoons ago, of an invitation to join big Connor in the basement of the Costa at the far end of the Walk for coffee. And what exactly was she doing in the Costa basement, surrounded by a dozen or so Goth kids meekly getting on with their homework, watching Connor stuff cheese and ham toasties into himself and check his mobile for Premier League news updates four times a minute? Basically, you hung out with people mostly because they were there, not because you relished their company, and because – unlike the denizens of the Bowthorpe flat – they were approximately your age and had some notion of the things you liked, or tolerated, or were prepared to put up with.

'What you doing on Saturday night then?' Connor asked, having finished his third toastie and fielded some more nonsense about Roy Hodgson getting the sack from Palace.

'Looking after my fucking kid. What are you doing?'

'Going to this club in Thetford. Could come if you want.'

'Fuck's sake, Connor.' And rather to her surprise, for these were intimate matters and not thus far even divulged to Carm, Jasmine found herself telling Connor about Louisa and the work experience and the big house at Taverham and what it might portend. Ten feet away the Goth kids were doing their customary trick of annoying the manager by sitting six to a table over one bottle of water and using the free wi-fi.

'Need your City and Guilds to do that,' Connor suggested, once the tale was told.

'City College,' Jasmine agreed. 'Three afternoons a week, Louisa said.'

'Your mum won't like that.'

No more she would, Jasmine thought, thinking it again now as she tugged the final shutter free of its moorings, discovered that the card machine had stopped working again and slashed the back of her right index finger open on the serrated edge of the Sellotape dispenser. The pink streaks in the sky were turning riper now and what looked like the Air Ambulance was heading west over the battlements of City Hall. There came the noise of a disturbance of the kind caused by two oversized people attempting to negotiate a confined space, and she turned round to find her mother and Barry bearing down on her. There was no doubt about it, Jasmine thought: they looked ridiculous. But then so much of what you saw around the place these days was ridiculous: the pale girls and their loaded prams coming back down London Street after a morning spent supporting their errant boyfriends at the Law Courts; the blue-blazered lads from the local private school with their lah-di-dah voices and plutocrat sports clobber; wherever you looked, absurdity ran rampant. There were worse sights than her mum and Barry moistly holding hands beneath the grey light of a Norwich morning. In fact, there were ways in which Barry and Carm represented a vote for stability, the old laws of modest comfort and low-key domesticity, fighting back against the clamour of the twenty-first century. Ten yards away Connor, staggering under the weight of a pile of saffron corduroys, was opening up his dad's stall, and she stood looking at him, wondering just what kind of bulwark he might be against the clamour of the twenty-first century, or whether, like most of the people you saw, in the end he was just himself, and that expecting anything else from him was as futile a pursuit as Barry's nightly vigil at the aquarium tank.

◊

On Wednesdays, which this was, Jasmine knocked off work early, collected little Bradley from the childminder's and wheeled him round to her nan's in Cadge Road. Here another set of protocols kicked in: the cautious unlocking of the double-bolted door; the squelching pad of nan's slippered

feet in transit over the moist lino; the treble-strength tea
served up in mugs commemorating Norwich City's triumph
in the 1985 Milk Cup; sliced-up Battenberg cakes on paper
plates. Unlike some people's grandmothers, who tended
to be bright young late-middle-aged things with toy-boy
fiancés saving up for holidays at Sharm-al-Sheik, Jasmine's
was properly old, old enough, she maintained, to remember the day the Second World War ended, and to recall a
time when the only non-white people you saw in Norwich
were the ones who came round selling clothes-pegs. Old
enough, too, to say the same things every week without ever
twigging that they might have been said before. This time
round it turned out to be family likenesses.

'Little Bradley,' Mrs Hood now pronounced, 'looks just
like his great-grandad.'

Privately Jasmine had her doubts about this, but there
was no stopping her nan once she got going.

'How's that then?'

'That red hair he's got. Just like his great-grandad.'

The only photograph of the late Mr Hood that Jasmine
had ever seen, taken in 1991, depicted a small, bald man
with a pair of caterpillar eyebrows. On the other hand,
she knew that old people had to be allowed their foibles.
Meanwhile, her nan had moved on to a more absorbing
topic.

'How's my daughter?'

Calling Carmilla 'my daughter' was one mark of the
latent antagonism that persisted between Mrs Hood and
her solitary child. Another was turning up late at family
clambakes and leaving early having disparaged the food.
A third was affecting not to hear the doorbell when Carm

called round. Jasmine wondered what to say about this for a bit, before deciding that the circumstances called for an unvarnished recitation of the truth.

'She's got a new bloke.'

'That Barry isn't it? No, you're all right darling,' Mrs Hood said, patting little Bradley on the forearm and managing to dislodge the spout of his milk-beaker with the same bold gesture. 'Works at the mall, I heard.' Nan's intelligence network extended beyond West Earlham to the City Centre and the debatable lands beyond. 'What's he like?'

What was Barry like? What was any middle-aged man who worked as a security guard, weighed 220 pounds and owned a tankful of miniature koi carp like? It was difficult to say. Jasmine wondered about replying that he was a lazy sod but that his solicitous attitude to her mother did him credit but decided to go with a non-committal 'he's all right.'

'Picks them, your mother does,' Mrs Hood said with exceptional savagery. 'How did you get on at that place at Taverham?' This, too, was unexpected as Jasmine didn't remember having told her about it.

'It was all right,' she volunteered.

'Well, you stick with that,' Mrs Hood said grimly, like some terrible old witch pronouncing judgment in a children's book. 'You go and make something of yourself.' Jasmine bowed her head, unresentfully but with resignation. From an early stage in her life all kinds of people – school-teachers, careers advisers, benefits supervisors – had been telling her to make something of herself, advice that would have been easier to follow if those delivering it had shown any awareness of the base materials out of which that making presumably had to be accomplished.

'Ever see that Ashley?' Mrs Hood went on, homing in on another weak spot.

'Not as such.' Jasmine conceded.

'Thought not,' Mrs Hood said, with a certain amount of not-very-well-concealed derision. 'You want some more Battenberg cake?'

But Jasmine, oppressed by the thought of a world in which she had to make something of herself and little Bradley was destined to grow up into a bald old man with caterpillar eyebrows, could only shake her head.

◊

It turned out that there was someone else who wanted her to make something of herself. This person was Connor, who, impressed by ongoing sales of the Taylor Swift mirrors and for some reason disaffected with his dad and the clothing concern, had proposed a commercial alliance, operating out of a newly vacant lot on the other side of the market next to the taxi-rank. 'Selling what, exactly?' Jasmine had demanded – a bit snappily – as they sat in the Costa basement again and Connor, tiring of the cheese toasties, was working his way through a pile of bacon baps, and Connor had said – a bit shyly – more of the kind of thing she was introducing to Carm's stall. 'My mum's really going to like that,' Jasmine demurred, even more snappishly – one of the discoveries she had made during the stake-outs in the Costa basement was that Connor was tolerant of female caprice; Ashley would already have told her to fuck off. 'Anyway, what about my City and Guilds?' 'Do that any time you like,' Connor said, meaning, she suspected, any time he liked, which might not be any time at all. 'Get the thing going and such.' 'Get the thing going and such,' Jasmine told him. 'Yeah.' She wondered what Connor would be like in charge of his own modest establishment, as opposed to being goaded and suborned by his weaselly old dad, and decided that he couldn't be worse than the Carm/Jasmine nexus under which she currently laboured. It was not that Barry actively interfered with the management of the stall, of which he had several times remarked to Carm that 'it's all yours, girl,' rather that he had a depressing habit of holding up items that caught his eye, regarding them mournfully and then saying 'These ain't shifting are they love?' while Carm stared mistily at him as if they were on some Channel Five consumer affairs show. Then there was the fact that he hung about the place eating chips, hello-darling the customers and trading off-colour banter with the shouty bloke who sold replica football shirts who he had adopted as his own particular friend.

And still it would have been all right, still it would have been OK – possibly – if it hadn't been for the morning when all these things suddenly tangled themselves up into a single, unpickable knot. It was about 8.30, with the shutters long down and the bit of the plastic apron adorning the stall's frontage that had fallen off tacked back on with a piece of Sellotape, and the sky a weird, bruising mackerel colour, and already the texts were flowing in: from Louisa wondering if she wanted another day's work experience and how the City and Guilds application was going, and from Ashley (*cld cum round with t@keout*)), and with the day's essentials firmly in place: the packet of fags open on the counter; Carm, pink-cheeked and wind-cheatered smoking one at her side; the shouty man bawling away two pitches down; Connor wandering down from his dad's stall every so often to give her the eye; the mingled odour of newly-delivered fish, root vegetables and cut-price perfume drifting on the early-spring air. Inspecting the row for signs of approaching trade, Jasmine found herself reviewing some of the triumphs and set-backs and attendant obligations of the past twenty-four hours: that little Bradley had taken what was indisputably a step or two over the cluttered carpet of the front room; that Barry's aquarium had sprung a nasty leak, temporarily fixed with a blob of chewing gum; that another sit-down with Connor about the vacant lot had proved inconclusive; that the City and Guilds form was still sitting in her shoulder-bag. For some reason the sight of Barry shambling into view with a cellophane package under his arm – he was wearing his security guard's uniform, which, mysteriously, made him look even less reliable than usual – did not disperse these fragments but somehow served to glue them together.

'I gossome masking tape,' Barry said, a faint tone of pride in his voice. 'Fix that plastic.;

'That's good then,' Jasmine said. She was still cross about Melanie ringing seven times last night (*'Barry . . . Barry love'*) and Barry setting off the smoke alarm by forgetting about his fucking toast.

'And that mate of mine says he can get us a deal on the new TV,' Barry went on, failing – as ever – to realise that he was getting the brush-off.

'You and your mates,' Jasmine said. Barry's mates were

every bit as unreliable as Barry himself. They propped up bars and traded dodgy electrical equipment, had names like Kev and Malky and were rarely present at any of the addresses where Barry turned up in the hope of seeing them. And then suddenly the pace of this hitherto desultory conversation speeded up.

'You home for your tea tonight then?' Carm fondly enquired. There had been some question of Barry attending a snooker tournament at the Fiveways.

'Might be. Might not be.'

'You ought to come back,' Carm wheedled. 'Come and have your tea. You know how little Bradley likes to see his Uncle Barry.'

'For Christ's sake, mum,' Jasmine said. 'He's not Bradley's Uncle Barry.'

Carmilla had a variety of facial expressions, amongst which the soppy look with which she regarded Barry; the vague look which set in after three Barcadi-and-Cokes; and the affronted look, when she imagined that her contribution to the bright, teeming world through which she wandered was being undervalued, all featured highly.

'Well at least he takes an interest in the kid. Unlike some people I could mention.'

Jasmine found that she was less annoyed by the 'some people I could mention' than the vision of Barry bending over little Bradley's cot.

'He can take all the interest he wants. I'm not having him called Bradley's Uncle Barry.'

'That's no way to talk to your mum,' Barry said uneasily.

'Why don't you fuck off?' Jasmine told him, alarmed but at the same time exhilarated by the sudden fury that reared up inside her. 'You and your fucking koi carp and your toast.'

'Here,' Barry said. 'Here now. Hang on.' His face was slowly crumpling up, as if all the seams were coming apart, 'Here now.' There were several things you did not do on Norwich market. One of them – unless you were the showman type – was to raise your voice above the standard barker's murmur. Another was to grab anyone – especially a woman – by the arm. If you did that then one of the onlooking market personnel would come and see what you were up to and, if necessary, sort you out. This time the vigilante was Connor, who, interrupting one of his regular saunters down the row, loomed up in front of the till and with surprising dexterity for a lad his size rapped Barry hard in the sternum. 'You young *cunt*,' Barry wailed, swung a fat fist, took another one on the point of his chin and went down in a heap. Carm, shrieking, thought about having a go, decided against it and instead bent down to attend to him while various other people who had been hanging around came up to offer advice.

And that should have been that. Only Jasmine, with Connor's big anaconda forearm pinioning her to his side and his hand in her hair and the sound of Barry's ghoul-summoned-from-the-vault breathing echoing in her ear, knew that it wasn't, that somehow a line had been crossed, that different destinies from the ones she had mapped out were in prospect, that somehow Connor would get his stall and her, and that it was impossible for her to resist, that she did not know what she wanted, or when it came to it – and this was the truly terrible thing – if she wanted anything at all.

Sea Palling

T HEY LEFT THE car in the second of the two overflow fields and then made their way to the piecemeal
agglomeration of snack bars and entertainment hutches a
hundred yards off to the right. Cross when he had been
manoeuvring the Volvo estate into its oblong of flattened
marram grass, Julian perked up at the sight of the rows
of Ford Fiestas and rusty camper vans. The girls, scampering at their side, were, as Martha quickly divined, far
more excited than they had been by any stage of the holiday so far. It was all a far cry from the seemly gastropubs
of Burnham Market and the genteel beaches beyond.
Reaching the start of the township, they came to a halt on
the verge and stood examining the dozen or so burger bars,
gift shops and amusement arcades that crowded round the
path to the dunes.

'Bit cheap and cheerful,' Julian suggested.

'Well, *I* like it,' Martha said. There had been one or two
occasions in the past when Julian had been so appalled by
his first glimpse of a likely-looking stopping-off point that
they had packed up and left on the spot. 'And so do the
girls. Look, you can see for yourself.'

'I'm not having them going in that penny arcade.'

But the girls, Hetty and Lyra, seemed more interested in a shop that sold sun hats and cheap plastic sunglasses. Watching them as they riffled through the trumpery items in the cardboard display box and feeling the first rays of sun on her ill-protected neck, Martha wondered how the day was going to turn out. Julian was clearly annoyed about something – it might have been the absence of fruit juice from the breakfast table, or it might have been the music from some unidentifiable distant source that kept them up in the night – and also more than normally self-conscious. He was on the shortish side and having to wear low-heeled espadrilles rather than the clumpy one-and-a-half inch brogues he usually strode around in was clearly weighing on his mind. As they watched the girls gambolling back from the gift joint, past a café garden where a quartet of over-sized women with huge mottled forearms sat companionably over cans of Tizer, he said:

'I heard from Alice Sutherland the other day. Apparently she and Greg are staying in this neck of the woods.'

'Oh yes.' Alice Sutherland, *née* Pargeter, was a name from the very old days, that spangled Oxbridge palisade that Martha could have done with not hearing quite so much about. 'I thought when they went on holiday it was by private jet to the Antilles or somewhere, with a butler to serve the tea.'

'They're not *that* rich. Anyway, I think her mother lives round here,' Julian said vaguely. There was still something preoccupying him that, Martha suspected, had nothing to do with the vagrant fruit juice, the small hours jingle-jangle, his height or the shooting star that was

Alice Sutherland burning through the night sky. 'Did you find anything good?' he demanded of Hetty as she came bounding into view. 'No,' Hetty said, who even at eleven seemed to know what looked good and what didn't. 'The sunglasses were all horrible.' Just then his mobile quivered and he fished it out of the pocket of his shorts.

'Sorry about this,' he said, without the least shred of regret. 'I just have to . . .'

Julian had a habit of leaving his sentences unfinished, presumably as a kind of challenge to his audience. 'Is it all right if we . . . ?' 'Would it be possible to . . . ?' Imperceptive listeners sometimes fell by the wayside, missed out on points of detail or alterations to schedule by dint of their inability to fill in the gaps. Listening to him murmuring about deferred capital gains and seven forty-sevenths applying – Julian was a corporate tax partner with one of the second-tier firms – Martha thought that she had heard worse. They had once walked the Quantocks with a phone-tethered medic who had turned out to be advising on a liver-transplant.

'Sorry,' Julian said again, returning the phone to his pocket with even less compunction than before, and she smiled back at him. Martha worked part-time for a firm that published up-market travel-guides, and no one in all the years she had laboured there had ever thought her worth ringing up on holiday. Julian's boss, on the other hand, was famous for having taken a client call on the summit of Mont Blanc. They were half-way along the path to the beach now and the wide sky was quite undifferentiated, a solid layer of blue on all sides.

'You see, girls,' Julian said, noting the sign that

prohibited dogs in the summer months, 'we couldn't have brought Hector anyway.'

'Do you think Hector gets sad in kennels?' Lyra wondered.

'No, I think he likes a change just as much as the rest of us,' Martha said, jinking her way around an enormous pile of excrement that some other Hector had left next to the overflowing litter bin and remembering that, like Julian, she, too, was cross about something that might have been the mention of Alice Sutherland and her fortunate husband, or the publishing firm's insistence on cutting her hours to two-and-a-half days a week, or the fact that Julian made so much money advising people on how to minimise their tax liabilities that there was no need for her to work at all. But the sight of the sea, at once inviting and glacial, cheered her up and she made an effort to keep pace with Hetty and Lyra as they rushed down to the water's edge. Julian, meanwhile, was losing his self-consciousness in a different way, laying out the blanket in an exact, unwavering square, settling the towels neatly on its topmost margin and then sitting carefully on it with his knees drawn up under his chin like a grasshopper and a rather puzzled expression on his face. The puzzled expression was one of the things Martha liked about him, as it seemed to denote an expertise that went only so far. He could drive them all from their holiday let in his Volvo estate and bask in telephone conversations about seven forty-sevenths applying, but after that occupation failed him.

'It's nice here,' she said, twenty minutes later, when the girls, now bikini-clad and lotion- besmeared, were amusing themselves by running into the sea as fast as they could and then running out of it screaming at the tops of their voices. 'I told you it would be.'

'The important thing is that everyone enjoys themselves,' Julian said with what could have been absolute sincerity or the untrammelled upper-middle-class Englishman's irony that always irked her so much. He was bored on holiday, but usually managed to disguise it. All this prompted her to consider the holidays of her youth, which had been much more modest affairs, undergone in caravans on seaside estates and consisting of long walks and chicken-in-a-basket meals in pubs. A part of her regretted their absence and the absence of some of the people who had shared the caravans with her, while another part was grateful to be staying a fortnight in a four-bedroom house with a two-acre garden, internet access and a village half-a-mile away with a proper butcher. There had been *longueurs* in those bygone vacations, just as there were *longueurs* now. The difference was that there had been no Julian, only her father falling asleep in deck-chairs and listening to the cricket on the radio.

Julian tipped the antique Panama hat he wore on beach holidays up from his knobby forehead. 'Let's go for a walk,' he said.

Another thing about Julian was his restlessness. If he was not actively prevented, he would probably go off and re-park the Volvo or suggest that they went somewhere else altogether. Even their honeymoon had been a dash through what seemed like several dozen picturesque Dordogne villages. And so they wandered off – or rather Martha wandered, the girls buzzed and Julian prowled furiously – eastward along the beach, past the rock pools and occasional family groups playing French cricket or hurling frisbees that the breeze caught and sent tumbling so far away into the blue sky that sometimes the throwers could not be bothered to fetch them back, and Martha thought, as she so often thought on these occasions, that Hetty and Lyra were, on the one hand, exactly as she had been as a child, and, on the other, weird, techno-suborned aliens, blown in from a world whose protocols she could barely comprehend. They had been walking for a good half mile, and she was gearing herself up to ask just exactly when they were going to have lunch and what it might consist of, when Julian suddenly came to a halt, tipped the Panama hat back up from his forehead again and said: 'Look who's here.'

There were half-a-dozen different pods of beach-go-ers within a radius of fifty yards, and she inspected them in turn, wondering if he meant the shiny woman in the scarlet bathing-costume, or the three small boys who had buried their father up to his neck in sand and were pelt-ing him with seaweed, or the elderly man who was trying to coax a bored-looking girl onto a fairy-cycle. But Julian was already in rapid and, she realised, deferential transit towards a woman with extravagant corn-coloured hair and a tall, oversized man who were camped on either side of a picnic basket in the shade of the dunes.

'Alice,' Julian was saying in that clipped but effusive voice of his. 'Greg. What a surprise.'

Was it a surprise? Martha wondered, as she came up wearily behind him. Julian was quite capable of proposing a trip to a beach in the secret knowledge that Alice and Greg might be in the vicinity, but looking at him as he crashed into view, with little rivulets of sand spilling over the tops of his espadrilles, she decided that it was simple happenstance. 'Julian,' Greg said courteously, 'Matty', and Martha stopped and stared at Alice's hair, which was even more luxuriant and artistically enhanced than before, noted the reading material set out beside the picnic-basket – *Financial Times, Economist, Spectator* – and registered, once again, the faint tremor of discomfort that stemmed not only from Greg being a director of Goldman Sachs while Julian laboured in chartered accountancy, and the thought of those far-off days on college lawns in which she had not herself participated, but from the fact that he was, by any reasonable standard of evaluation, such a colossal idiot.

'I do like that sundress, Matt,' Alice was saying, one hand firmly clasped to the lid of the picnic basket as if she feared that whatever lay inside it might try to escape. 'It really suits you.' Another thing about the Sutherlands was that neither of them ever called her by her proper name. Who knew? By the time they said goodbye Greg would probably start addressing her as 'Marty.' Looking at him as he stood up, smoothing grit off his python-sized forearms and demonstrating that he did not really have the figure for the genitalia-hugging pouch that did service for a swimming costume, Martha wondered, as she quite often did, how, in a supposedly meritocratic age, people like Greg managed to prosper in the world. 'Oh, Greg's a dark horse,' Julian had said, when this opinion had been tentatively conveyed to him. 'I mean, there was one term at college where he did no work at all. Absolutely none. And then in the very last tutorial he read out an essay about feudalism that Dr Metcalfe said was the most brilliant thing he'd ever heard in thirty years of teaching.'

'Where are the children?' she heard herself saying brightly. 'How did you manage to escape them?'

'Grandma,' Greg said, holding a finger to the side of his nose. 'Would you believe she's taken them to Yarmouth Pleasure Beach? There's a game old girl if ever I saw one.'

'Hetty. Lyra,' Alice said, in a kindly way. 'You're simply enormous. Twice as big as when I last saw you. I hope you're enjoying school. You must tell me all about it.'

The other thing about Greg, Martha reflected, as he and Julian embarked on a forthright and, it seemed to her, performative discussion of some piece of recent business news, was how on earth he had persuaded Alice to marry him. On the other hand, it had to be acknowledged that there were plenty of women of her acquaintance hooked up to complete stiffs, detecting hidden depths where others found only an all-encroaching shallowness. Judging that Alice was entirely sincere in wanting to hear about school, the girls immediately sat down at her side and began to talk with immense formality about matters which Martha discovered, to her horror, she knew little of herself. This was disquieting, as was the paralysing heat, the realisation that what she particularly desired on this bright August day, and despite her all-consuming love for her daughters, was to be on her own somewhere reading a book, and the snatches of pompous conversation drifting back from Greg and Julian's side of the picnic basket. Had they been like this at Cambridge? She had a vision of Julian ferrying drinks back from the bar, or filling Greg in on lecture timetables he hadn't bothered to consult. Julian, she thought, with the realism she managed to bring to their shared life about six or seven times a year, left a lot to be desired, but deep down he was all right, morally sound and approachable in a way that Greg manifestly wasn't. All of which made their long association – Greg had been best man at the wedding – not so much inexplicable, for she had her own dealings with bores and lunatics and treacherous half-friends, but worth considering for the clues it might offer to Julian and his own personality.

'What it all hangs on,' Greg was saying, brow slightly furrowed and lashing out at a wasp with the now rolled-up copy of the *Financial Times*, 'is Corporation Tax not going up.'

'I hear what you're saying,' Julian said, who, as Martha knew, had strong views on Corporation Tax, 'but it . . .'

'Nonsense,' Greg countered. 'That's what you tax people always say.'

There were, as Martha knew, other sides to Greg. There was, however hard it might be to believe it, a Greg who dressed up as Santa at children's parties. There was a Greg who had written her quite a nice letter after her father died. And there was also a Greg who lashed effortfully at wasps with a rolled-up copy of the *FT* and stood on Sea Palling beach as if every grain of sand had been placed there with the express intention of feeding his sense of self-satisfaction.

'Oh, I know what I meant to say,' Greg said about twice as loudly as anyone else would have done when the person they were talking to was a bare three feet away. 'Guess who we're having dinner with tonight?'

It would be that sodding actress called Sukie someone they always talked about, the appearance of whom without her top in a student revue had apparently been the height of their undergraduate careers, Martha thought, or the wheedling goblin who sometimes turned up on the lunch-time news in his role as a junior Treasury minister. On the other hand, she had an idea from the proud look on Greg's face that he had landed an even bigger fish.

'Jimmy Mackintosh.'

'I thought they spent August in the Hamptons?' Julian said.

'Actually, no. Jimmy's turned into an eco-warrior. Strange but true. He's bought an estate over in Suffolk. And every time he makes a killing he goes and plants another hundred trees.'

The girls had stopped telling Alice about their school and were giving her the run-down on Hector. Here again, Martha found that she was being fed bits of information that were new to her.

'How is the old sod?' Julian enquired in a tone that, for all its old-chums-together jauntiness, ended up seeming just the tiniest bit wistful.

'Well, he's making a lot of money,' Greg said. 'The place in Suffolk looks as if Jay Gatsby ought to be walking around in it.'

Martha searched her memory for another face on the freshers' photo that still hung in the corridor upstairs and finally identified her target. If Sukie was the one who had taken her top off at the college revue, and Dominic was the one who had ended up as a Treasury minister, then Jimmy was the one who was famous for amassing some unimaginable amount of money – a million pounds? Ten million pounds? – before his twenty-fifth birthday and been profiled in the *Sunday Times* business section. He ran a hedge fund and his financial activities, when outlined to the lay-person, sounded surprisingly like a kind of high-end Monopoly.

'Why don't you ring him up and see if Julian and Marts can come?' Alice said, surfacing from the rapt account of Hector's distemper. 'He'd love to see them.'

'I could do that,' Greg said, a bit uncertainly, like a singer taking requests from an esoteric back-catalogue. 'I could do that.'

'Oh he won't want to see us,' Julian said hastily.

'Yes he will. You can talk to him about Corporation Tax. I don't suppose he's ever paid a penny of it in his life, but he'll be interested to hear.'

Martha realised that she was not listening to Greg, Julian and Alice anymore, but looking at the beach as it stretched out before her. It was not that there was anything in particular going on, and what there was she could have happily have done without. In fact, to her exacting eye the place would have been vastly improved if Greg could somehow have been removed from it. But mysteriously, the sand and the water beyond it, in which a kayak or two were going determinedly by and container ships lay static on the horizon, held her gaze, and she knew that, left to her own devices, she would have liked to set off on a long, shambling run to the water's edge, waving her arms and yelling at the top of her voice as the children had done.

Seeing that no one had actively tried to dissuade him, Greg plucked his phone dramatically from the pocket of his shirt and stalked off along the beach. For a moment or two time seemed to hang suspended in the air. The kayaks were

long gone and the container ships were motionless, like
pieces of painted scenery in a play. The girls, bored by all
this grown-up talk, had started to play grandmother's footsteps in the sand. Alice, meanwhile, was sitting cross-legged
on the blanket, showing off her splendid calves and emit-
ting one of her gracious Madonna-and-infant smiles. The
heat was even less supportable than it had been when they
set out, and Martha realised that where she really wanted
to be was in a fantasy version of that superior clothes shop
in Holt they had visited earlier in the week, the doorway
lost in dense hummocks of shadow and fans blowing gently
overhead, trying on an endless series of dresses, all of which
fitted her, so that garment after garment lay on the chair at
her side, every one of which Julian was apparently eager to
pay for. Delighted by this phantasm, she basked in it until
the moment when Greg finished his phone call and came
lurching back into earshot.

'It's no go, I'm afraid. Jimmy says he's terribly sorry, but
he's got outside caterers in or something and they can't fit
any more seats round the table.'

'Never mind,' Julian said, who, as Martha well knew,
minded quite a bit.

'He's got Kwasi Kwarteng coming or someone,' Greg
said, as if this would somehow sweeten the pill.

'I should be jolly thankful you've got out of that one,
Matty,' Alice said, with what Martha suspected was a
genuine solicitude. 'You've never seen anything so boring
as those dinners Jimmy Mackintosh gives. I take a book
sometimes and read it under the table.'

'Hadn't we better go and see how your mother's getting
on with the bambinos?' Gregg wondered.

'I expect she's getting on splendidly,' Alice said. 'But yes, it would be a nice gesture.'

And so, by degrees, they drifted back along the beach, which seemed considerably larger than it had been on the outward journey, and began to climb the path through the dunes. A breeze had got up now, blown down from the fjords or the Russian steppe, and the air, though cooler, was scented with barbecue smoke. Martha wondered what they were going to do that afternoon and whether it might involve a craft shop, a tea shop or, ideally, a combination of the two, or whether they would end up going to the bird reserve at Titchwell again.

'Shame about Jimmy,' she said.

'Can't be helped,' Julian said. They had reached a part of the path where the soft sand spilled over your feet as you walked and he looked even shorter than ever. Enormous, wicked-looking herring gulls hung in the air along with the Nordic ozone and the stink of lighter fuel, and she reached out and laid a hand on his shoulder, which, after all, was what wives were supposed to do in such situations, and got back a look which might have been proudly-borne resignation, or cautious annoyance, or some other emotion, raw but unquantifiable, which she was simply unable to interpret, drifting off into the dense East Anglian sky. Back at the holiday township an ambulance had arrived to attend an old lady who had collapsed in the entrance to the amusement arcade and the third of the overflow fields beyond the car park was nearly three-quarters full.

Yare Valley Mud

THE ONLY TIME it was properly quiet in the Abacab office was around 4 a.m. At 3 there were still lairy kids shimmying along the Prince of Wales Road and chucking beer cans at the parked cars. Come 5 the account work started up and there were punters to take to Stansted and medical types to collect from the Norfolk & Norwich night-shift. But at 4 . . . Well now, at 4 things calmed down. The phones stopped ringing, the din from the clubs fell silent, the last of the beer monsters had been scraped off the pavement by an obliging constabulary and there was only him and Darren, sitting in the first-floor rabbit-hutch, upper bodies silhouetted in the sodium glare of the street-lamp, eyes out on stalks, cigarette smoke unfurling above their heads, staring out over the empty, rain-moistened streets. Him and Darren, drinking bitter black coffee out of the machine, hearing the click of the front door a dozen feet below, the sound of trainered feet on the uncarpeted stair, and wondering just who the fuck it could be wanting a cab at this unearthly hour, long before there were surgeons needing transit to operating tables and blokes with attaché cases off to breakfast meetings in Amsterdam. Because at 4 a.m. you never quite knew whose head would come bouncing up in front of the wire grille that enclosed the booking desk. Sometimes it would be a weaselly character in a suit lately decanted from the lap-dancing establishment down the way. Other times it would be some wretched girl with pinwheel eyes who'd probably passed out in a doorway and woken up wondering where exactly the fuck she was. This time, though, it was just a fat kid in a tee and those ridiculous plugged ear-lobes, shaking rain-water off his head all over the lino.

'Yeah, right,' Terry said, who in the absence of the plug-earrings and the little pool of water on the lino would probably have said: 'Where to, pal?'

'Taxi to Watton.'

'Taxi to Watton *please*.'

'Are you taking the piss?' the fat kid wanted to know.

'Come on, son,' Darren said, getting up from behind the desk so the fat kid could appreciate the full extent of his considerable bulk. 'You're not going to get a cab to Watton at this time of night. Twenty-three miles, that is. Won't be anyone around for an hour, if that.'

Strictly speaking, this was not accurate. In fact, as they both knew, a driver named Big Trevor was at this very moment parked up on Castle Meadow, a quarter of a mile away. On the other hand, when Darren took a dislike to someone you tended to let him have his head.

'Cost you fifty quid and all,' Darren said stonily. 'This time of night.' What management referred to as the small-hours fare structure was inclined to flexibility. Sometimes it was one-and-a-half times standard; sometimes it was double; you took your chance. The bluster was going out of the fat kid, who now looked as if he was about fifteen and lucky to have been allowed out in the first place.

'All right, son,' Terry said, a bit more emolliently. 'Know what I'd do if I were you? I'd head for the bus station and treat yourself to a cup of tea at the all-nighter. There's a Number 4 at 6.30 . . . Well, around that time,' Terry added, thinking that in actual fact it might be nearer 7.20.

Together they watched the fat kid's helmet of scurfy marmalade hair recede down the staircase. 'What was all that about?' Terry wondered as the click of the door resounded in the dead air.

'Can't stand those lairy kids,' Darren said, which was fair enough. In fact, no one at Abacab could stand those lairy kids, who had a habit of being sick all over the waiting area and thinking you could get five of their mates plus three bags of take-out into a standard-size minicab. 'Hey. It's 4.15.'

There was an unwritten agreement among the night staff that if nothing very much was doing you could shut down the office at 5, preparatory to the arrival of Becks and the morning staff at 6, but like the small-hours fare structure this inclined to flexibility.

'Hey,' Terry said, mock-ingenuously. 'Hang on. Hang on there. Could be a couple of rugby teams wanting to get back to Pontypridd. You never know.'

'Could be fuck all. Where are the keys?'

The keys were run to earth underneath the ripped-up sports pages of the previous day's *Eastern Evening News* ('Wagner faces fan fury.') Cautiously scenting the night air, which as usual smelled of kebab fat, weed and petrol fumes, they stepped out into the street. Normally at this time they went their separate ways – Terry back to his bachelor shakedown in Hall Road, Darren to connubial bliss with Maxine on the Heartsease estate – but this particular morning Darren had other ideas.

'Hey,' he said, one meaty hand tugging at the zip of an outsize Parka festooned with Mod regalia. 'You want to go to the Iceberg?'

The Iceberg was an after-hours club round the corner in Rose Lane, which stayed open until 6 a.m. and catered for participants in what the local paper called the 'night-time economy.' Bar-girls, doormen and persons such as themselves predominated. It was OK once in a while but you didn't want to make a habit of it.

'Just the one,' Darren said, sensing his disquiet. 'Just the one and we'll fuck off home.'

The Iceberg's premises were so inconspicuously situated that you could sometimes fail to locate the doorway, but Darren, an experienced voyager through the small-hours Norwich backstreets, had them there in a couple of minutes, with a spilled refuse sack that was clogging up the club's arid portal the only casualty. Inside it was just the same as ever, the speakers relaying cocktail jazz from somewhere deep in the last century, Sinatra and the Rat Pack staring down from lime-coloured walls and a couple of – no offence – burglar's dogs grimly conferring at the bar. Darren, the double brandies almost lost within his massive fists, kicked two chairs to within touching distance of the nearest table, and announced, with infinite weariness:

'New bloke was in the other afternoon, Becks said.'

So this was what Darren wanted to talk about. 'Oh yeah? What he want?'

'What do new owners ever want? Becks said he was just sniffing about. You know, going through the booking files and such.'

The brandy, as was customary at the Iceberg, tasted of hair-oil. 'Well, he won't find anything in the booking files. Who is he anyway?'

'Some fucker called Abercrombie,' Darren said bitterly. 'Don't suppose he's ever driven a cab in his life.'

They sat and drank the terrible brandy and contemplated the spectacle of fuckers called Abercrombie who had never driven a cab in their lives going through the booking files, which was basically what you did in the Iceberg in the hour before it shut. Outside the noise of the traffic was increasing. Soon, Terry knew, it would be dawn, with all the horror that entailed: the spectral drive back through the rain-swept city; the buses starting to clog up the arterial roads; all that fugitive human life suddenly in motion. Over at the bar a low-level debate about some absent third party that had been chuntering on since they had sat down came to a climax and the larger of the two girls raised her voice to a squawk, the better to press home some reputation-shredding point. 'Jesus,' Darren said, hoisting himself up from the table and getting his blitzed red eyes into focus. 'Buy you ladies a drink?'

Terry knew how it worked here: Darren's chat-ups; Darren's extra-curricular women; the consequences for his domestic life back on the Heartsease estate – all this was legendary. He slapped a £5 note on the table to cover his share of the brandy, skipped down the stairs – funny how you could do a twelve-hour shift in the Prince of Wales Road and still not feel tired – and stood in the Iceberg's doorway watching the early lorries tear up Rose Lane to the King Street traffic lights, and in the distance the cathedral spire rearing towards the cloud canopy like a vicious steely dart.

◊

'Jesus,' Mr Abercrombie said, ten hours later, 'this place could do with a clean-up. I mean, I know they're only toe-rags off the street waiting for a cab, but they've still got to fucking sit here until it comes.'

Mr Abercrombie was a short, disillusioned man with a twitching gait and a grey complexion and, to be honest, not your usual owner of a mini-cab concern. 'I mean,' he went on, making an extravagant gesture with the fingers of his right hand that took in the winded sofa and the battered drinks machine that were the principal ornaments of the Abacab office, 'would it hurt anyone to run a Hoover over the carpet once in a while? That sofa,' Mr Abercrombie went on, warming to his theme, 'smells as if somebody died on it. Pissed themselves on it, anyhow.'

Terry and Darren traded the shifty, give-nothing-away glances that you customarily exchanged when new owners were making their presence felt, safe in the knowledge that it would all blow over and that normal standards of torpor would soon reassert themselves.

'All I'm asking,' Mr Abercrombie said wearily, all I'm fucking asking is that someone makes an effort. We're not running a fleet of stretch limos on Hollywood Boulevard. We've not got Mel fucking Gibson coming up the stairs, I accept that. But, you know, an *effort*.' Then, unexpectedly, his mood changed. 'I expect you lads have been here a long time. Am I right?'

Well, that was true enough, Terry acknowledged. Both he and Darren had indeed been there a very long time. Was it twenty-two years or twenty-three since they'd first signed on for Canary Cabs? Well, whatever it was they'd seen it: driving paralytic footballers back to their hotels for £20 tips; watching the riot vans barrelling down the Prince of Wales; ferrying the disabled kids up to Cromer for their Charity Day; every scene, incident and calamity that the taxi-driving life could offer.

'Hell of a long time,' Darren conceded.

'Yeah, well,' Mr Abercrombie said, all trace of cheeriness gone. 'Expect we'll get along just fine. Anything else I ought to know?'

'Fucking council's making a song and dance about the parking again.'

'Oh yeah, I heard about that. You go and license a mini-cab firm to – what is it? ' *ply its trade*, and then you start charging them for parking up outside. I mean,' Mr Abercrombie went on savagely, 'who gives a fuck about the small businessman, eh? The people who keep the infrastructure going? OK, that'll do for now. Here, you – Terry is it? Do me a favour tomorrow morning. Get round to the house for 11 and take my wife to the airport, will you?'

'You want to watch him,' Darren said, as the slam of Mr Abercrombie's car door sounded in the street below. 'Thin end of the fucking wedge, that is. Next thing you know he'll have you driving his kids to school or bringing his old mum down from Birmingham, or whatever.'

'I've had worse,' Terry told him. There had been

previous owners who had insisted that their employees trim lawns, check out gutters and one occasion erect a fairly substantial gazebo in their back garden. Driving some-one's wife to the airport was pretty low on the scale. The switchboard, blithely ignored while they were attending to Mr Abercrombie, had started winking away, so Darren jabbed at the nearest light and picked up the intercom. Terry listened sympathetically to the brisk conversation that followed ('Yes mate . . . No mate . . . I've told you mate, you're fucking banned you are . . .') and clapped his hands appreciatively a couple of times. 'Was that the bloke from Earlham Road?' 'Actually no, it was the bloke from the Bowthorpe.' *'Him?* I thought he'd been banged up.' 'Apparently not,' Darren said. 'Still at leisure.' He looked suddenly grim and ground down, but at the same time fizzing with energy, as if an electrical charge had started pulsing through his limbs, and Terry, who could read the signs and knew what these tremors of agitation meant, wondered how long it would be before he went off on one again, and what the consequences for Darren and himself and Mr Abercrombie and everyone else in the immediate vicinity might be.

◊

The Abercrombies lived in a big house off the Thorpe Road. Mrs Abercrombie, flame-haired, lissom, five foot ten and a good fifteen years younger than her husband, was standing on the doorstep when he arrived, one long, leather-booted foot propped up on her suitcase..

'Are you Terry?' she asked as she got into the back of the

cab, a moist hand lingering on the door-frame as he held it open. 'Nick was telling me about you. And that bloke you work with. Said you were a right pair of divots.'

'Yeah, right,' Terry said. 'Airport is it?'

They rode in silence through the placid mid-morning streets while Mrs Abercrombie – Frankie – sent and received text messages, phoned someone called Lauren who might have been her sister or, alternatively, was advising her on the refurbishment of her kitchen, and gorged on extra-strong mints. As they came in through Hellesdon, curiosity got the better of him and he said:

'Where are you off to then?'

'Newcastle,' Frankie said. 'Stay with my friend. See the sights. She lives in Gosforth. Her husband's a footballer.'

'Who's he play for?' Here in Norwich you only got the City squad and an occasional Ipswich interloper manifestly out of their comfort zone.

'I don't know. What do I care?' They were in sight of the airport now; a spindly twin-propeller job bound for the Bacton gas terminal buzzed overhead. She held up ten glinting finger-nails in front of her and inspected them proudly. 'What's it like, driving a cab?'

What was it like driving a cab? The obvious answer was that it was about the customers and their vagaries. Sometimes there were people who wanted to talk to you about themselves, and sometimes there were people who wanted you to talk to them about yourself. Sometimes there were people who had some hobby-horse they wanted to climb onto and simply ranted – it could be about Brexit, or the pot-holes on the A47 or the fluoride in the water – while you sat there, hands gripping the wheel and occasionally checking out the distended, plum-coloured face in the mirror. Sometimes there were people – old people, mostly – who were so lonely they simply wanted you to ferry them around Norwich for a couple of hours for the company. Sometimes there were edgy blokes with shell-shocked faces who you kept an eye on in case they decided to kick off. Other times, though, coming back from contract jobs or trips through the beet fields, it wasn't about the customers at all. No, those times it was about other things – the view out of the window, the silence in the cab or what seemed like silence until you remembered the hum of the engine. There you would be, out on the Acle Straight with the dawn coming up, or somewhere on the road to Lynn with not another car in sight, or maybe just a container lorry looming up in the distance, and rain falling over the grey fields, and you'd feel . . . Well, what exactly would you feel? That there were worse places to be than in a cab coming through the Norfolk countryside at sunrise with the sky going from pink to grey and the streams of freezing fog buffeting the windscreen. That is, until you got back to base to discover that three people had phoned in sick, you were working a double shift and your next job was taking a deaf old lady off to visit her sister in Luton.

'You get all sorts,' he said after a bit.

'I bet you do.'

By the time he'd dropped her off at the airport, wheeled her suitcase up to the check-in counter and stood gallantly by as she burrowed for the ticket in her shoulder bag, he had a definite feeling that he was being given the eye. Evidence for this deduction could be found in the way she'd leaned into him while he was trundling the suitcase, the way the moist hand had rested once more on the door-frame as she got out of the car and the considerable amount of stockinged thigh exposed to view while this manoeuvre was being attempted.

'I'll see you again,' she said as he took his leave. It sounded more like a threat than an invitation.

'Daresay you will.'

Disquieting as this suspicion was, it was altogether eclipsed by the news that Darren had managed to procure the girl from the Iceberg's phone number and that she was 'well up for it.'

'What's she doing at the Iceberg then?' It was early evening and they were back in the office wondering how many drivers were going to turn up and suspecting that it might be two short.

'Works at the Sherbet Dip.'

'Pole-dancing place, that is. Champagne at ten quid the glass. Sammy said he went round there one night and they wouldn't let him in for not wearing a tie.'

'It's not pole-dancing. It's more artistic. Comes on with a load of silk scarves and that.'

You could never tell Darren he was being an idiot. It was like telling Donald Trump that the democratic process wasn't really his kind of thing. Terry shortened the focus of his eyes to take in the room beyond them and in doing so noticed something that had previously escaped his attention.

'What the *fuck* is that?'

Darren let his hand stray onto the sofa's glossy leather, or at any rate high-end imitation glossy leather surface in rather the same way that Frankie had allowed her fingers to rest on the door of Terry's cab.

'Come in this morning from the Furniture Warehouse, this did. While you was off taking her ladyship to the airport.

'*Christ!*' Terry said, genuinely shocked by these intimations of change, decay and disturbance.

'I know,' Darren told him, who Terry could see was still cross about the pole-dancing. 'Pearls before bleeding swine.'

◊

But change, it had to be said, was endemic to the world Terry seemed to be living in. You could see it in the way the chain stores in the malls were all morphing into charity shops; you could see it in the flocks of *Big Issue* sellers, who had stopped being old blokes from the Night Shelter and turned into plump girls with ten-carat teeth from the Carpathians, and you could see it in the ebb and flow of your professional day-to-day. Half the time Terry peered through a cab windscreen as it whisked by he saw an unfamiliar and occasionally ethnic minority face. Not that Terry had anything against the foreign boys. No, they were top lads, most of them. But they didn't have the knowledge, the heft, the *expertise*. Even with a satnav they'd end up every so often in some ditch in Blofield wondering how they'd missed the road to North Walsham, with the punter phoning base on his mobile to ask what the fuck was going on. Yet more disquieting, Terry could see it in his private life, what with Frankie and her phone calls and the lure of the big house off the Thorpe Road.

Even before it started, he knew how it was going to go, how it would play out, and even – he suspected – how it would end. There had been other Frankies – not exactly bosses' wives, but strung-out women with time on their hands and roving eyes. You either sailed in there and did what they wanted or you kept well away. As for the preliminaries – not that they amounted to very much – Terry could have ticked the list off on the back of a postcard: the fake errands; the husband in Leicester, where Mr Abercrombie went in pursuit of the wide range of business interests that were his to command; the breathy phone calls to base. His first idea was that she was trying to get one back on her husband, but a couple of weeks' intimacy convinced him that personal spite had nothing to do with it and that this was just the way she carried on. She was a big, slatternly girl who left biscuit crumbs on every surface within a ten-foot radius and looked at her mobile even when they were in bed. When they'd finished in there, and if the weather was fine, they'd sit on the decking that had been erected behind the French windows looking at the long oblong of garden and the river that flowed beyond it.

'Must be nice, living by the water,' he said on one of these occasions.

'Fucking liability,' Frankie explained. 'Every time it rains the bottom end turns into a marsh and there's a plague of fucking frogs or whatever. Where do you live, anyway?'

'Hall Road,' he told her, omitting to mention the two students and the harassed Asian couple also quartered beneath the establishment's sagging roof.

'*Hall Road*? I'm not coming there.'

Sometimes, though, it was all right. Sometimes it really was OK. One afternoon they went to Winterton, ostensibly to look at the seals, discovered that the beach café had been washed into the sea and ended up in a tea shop in Martham, sitting in a companionable silence broken only by the ping of Frankie's phone going off. Another time they took her ridiculous little toy dog for a walk around Thorpe Rec and watched it dash off in terror every time a pigeon came within five yards. All the while, though, like Darren in the office above the Prince of Wales Road, she was ready to kick off, spoiling for a fight, if not with him then whoever else lay to hand.

'I hate this place,' she said at the tea shop in Martham.

'What's wrong with it?' He assumed she meant the shop, which was a genteel concern with willow-pattern crockery and fancy doilies on the table-tops.

'No, not here. What's outside. Cows in fields. All these slow people. All that fucking *wind*. City girl, I am.'

He itemised a few of the local amenities – Norwich's two cathedrals, the fifty pubs was it?, the twin shopping malls – but it was no good.

'It's not like Leicester,' she said, which would have been half-way funny had she not meant it so seriously.

From elsewhere there came signs that others among them were feeling the pace. When he got back to the office it was to find that a row of expensive-looking cane-back chairs had been installed in the waiting-area together with a poster informing anyone who happened to be sitting in them that the management valued their custom and were anxious to serve them at all times.

'Load of old bollocks,' Darren said, setting down the back page of the *Eastern Evening News* ('Kenny: "Our Luck Has to Change".') He was wearing one of his big leather jackets, the shiny surface so unyielding that it you took it off and put it on the sofa it sat there like a suit of armour, and looked even more terrifying than usual.

'How's that girl from the Dip? The Goddess Volumnia or whatever her name is.'

'Can watch your fucking mouth, you can,' Darren said feelingly. 'Actually mate, it's a fucking nightmare.'

And this, Terry had to admit, was a point worth making. Because all relationships these days tended to be nightmares. It wasn't that the people involved didn't like you, or didn't want to be with you, or – with occasional exceptions – had gone into the business with the express intention of mucking you about. No, it was just that they all came with baggage – chunky, obtrusive baggage that got in the way, so that sometimes it was as if you were trying to reclaim your suitcase from an airport carousel while a torrent of other cases cascaded down on it out of the chute. For a start, everyone – even the fresh-faced kids in their twenties – had half-a-dozen exes hanging around the place, and sometimes a baby or two in some comfortless council flat up the Aylsham Road. Worse, the exes tended to be malign, vengeful and interfering, while the malignity and the vengefulness were everywhere abetted by technology. Even Frankie, who of all the women he'd ever met seemed the best able to look after herself, had some skank Instagrammer from a former life sending pictures of her round the internet.

'Hear what you're saying, mate.'

Darren shook his head. And that was another thing about the modern-day world of dalliance, the fact that it always seemed to involve betrayal, backstabbing and duplicity. Actually Terry didn't blame Darren for trifling with the affections of the Goddess Volumnia or whatever her name was. In fact, the Archbishop of Canterbury, if invited to inspect Darren's domestic arrangements, would probably have given him a free pass. And how did that make him feel about Mr Abercrombie and the besmirch-ment of his marital bed? Well, you took your chances and other people took theirs, or had them denied. It was as simple, or as complicated, as that.

'Some fucking ex-boyfriend sticking his nose in,' Darren went on. He looked sad and bewildered, like some vast creature of the deeps unexpectedly fetched up on dry land and wondering whether the natives were friendly.

It was about half-past four now, which meant that the first wave of homeward-bound office-workers would soon be infesting the premises. Sure enough, two minutes later a kid in a badly-fitting suit waltzed up the stairs, ordered a cab to Brundall and then flopped down on the sofa.

'Not on that, mate.' Darren said, a sudden light of menace in his eye.

'Why not?' The kid's eyebrows went up in puzzlement. 'There's a fucking sign there says you're anxious to serve me.'

'Can't sit on the sofa,' Darren told him severely. 'Can't sit on the sofa cos it's *new*.'

◊

A week later – they were getting on into the spring now, and a world of equinoctial gales and harassed weather-men – it began to rain. Real Norfolk rain, too, which if it got going at tea-time would still be pulsing away at dawn and would have had Noah rounding up every spavined wildebeest and gecko he could find, no question. 'That you, Tel?' Mr Abercrombie enquired, phoning in from Leicester four days after the heavens opened – he'd turned all matey of late and started calling them 'Tel' and 'Dazza'. 'Do me a favour will you and get up to Thorpe and give Mrs A. a hand'

'What kind of hand would that be?' Terry wondered. He hadn't seen Frankie for several days, for the compelling reason that the last time she had told him that he was a fucking loser who lived in a house with a load of tosser students

'How should I know?' Mr Abercrombie sounded distant, vague, not his usual bunchy self. 'Rung up in a state. Reckoned the river had burst its banks. Some fucking *flood* or other. You just get round there, Tel, and give her a hand.'

There was a milk float on its side north of the station and a couple of police cars holding up the traffic, so it took him half an hour to get to Thorpe. But Mr Abercrombie had been right about the flood. In fact, half the river seemed to have ended up in the back garden, from which vantage point it had swamped the decking, seeped through the French windows, deposited what looked like a sack full of silt on the fluffy white carpet and wrecked the three-piece suite. The front door was open and, walking inside, he discovered Frankie sitting on her haunches with a kind of improvised turban on her head and a squeegee mop in one hand, trying to decant dirty water into a bucket and not, it had to be allowed, making much of a job of it.

'River Yare,' he said, thinking some explanation was needed. 'Burst its banks'

'I know the river's burst its fucking banks. Christ, this suite cost £3,000.'

Happily he had experience in this kind of crisis. While she traipsed about dabbing at the pools of water with her squeegee mop he opened the French windows – the rain had stopped now – saw the river was in retreat and swept up some of the mud. Then he rang a bloke he knew who had an industrial dryer and solicited a quote. By the time he'd finished, most of the dirt was back out on the lawn, leaving a rank smell that suggested raw sewage.

'Not much more I can do,' he said. 'Lenny'll be round later with the dryer. You got insurance?'

'How would I know whether I've got insurance? Hey,' she said, when he was half-way to the door. 'This room smells like a fucking *toilet.*'

He found himself wondering what Mr Abercrombie would say when he got back from Leicester, to whose amenities he was apparently partial. Would he comfort the wife of his bosom? Would he bawl her out for not noticing sooner (Frankie had slept in late and not come downstairs until most of the damage was done)? Or would he simply fade into the fabric of the house? One of the oddest thing about the big house in Thorpe, it turned out, was how little trace of the owner's personality seemed to be contained in it.

'Keep the windows open,' he advised. 'Lenny'll be able to help.' This, as it happened, was a guess. Lenny had an industrial dryer, but was in other respects an idle sod. Sewage disposal was not one of his strong-points.

'You know what?' she said. 'I've had it up to here with this.' And he was sharp enough to know that she meant him as well as the stinking carpet, the soggy furniture and the River Yare.

Back at the office he learned that it had all gone tits up with the Goddess Volumnia, or whatever her name was. There was anguished mention of somebody called Jason.

◊

And there was something else that irked him, stole up on him when he least expected it and ground him down. The old Norwich faces: what had happened to them? Twenty years ago you saw them on every corner. Old blokes with features that looked as if they'd been carved out of balsa wood stepping confidently off kerbs into flowing traffic; old women with nutcracker chins off the bus from Wymondham or Attleborough with a fibrous shopping bag in each hand; skinny, undernourished kids off the estates dawdling into town on a Saturday forenoon to drift incuriously around the alleyways and queue up uncomplainingly outside Pizza Hut. A Pizza Hut, more to the point, that wasn't there any more. So where were they all, anyhow, the old blokes, and the women and the pale, scrawny boys? It wasn't as if they'd stopped existing, just that there didn't seem to be so many of them. Perhaps they'd gone somewhere else, found other bolt-holes, moved off to more hospitable climes without telling anyone where they'd gone. Whatever the explanation was, Terry found himself missing them. Meanwhile, they were building houses up in Rackheath on the field where he and Darren had gone rabbiting when they were kids. Whichever way you looked at it, Norwich was gone.

◊

And then came that terrible evening – well, early morning actually – when all these disparate threads were brought together in a single point of focus. Middle of the week, just before 4 a.m. and, once again, nothing doing. There'd been a kerfuffle outside at about 3.30 when a bunch of herberts in hoodies and trackie bottoms had up-ended a refuse bin into the doorway of the solicitors' office over the way, but the sound of a police van skidding its brakes as it arrived in the layby twenty yards down had sent them scurrying like frightened fowl. Four a.m. and nothing much doing. Not a call for the last half-hour. Darren with his head down on the desk. Terry eating the remains of a kebab that someone had brought in an hour back. Darren gave a start, came awake and reached for the cigarette packet in what was virtually the same instant.

'When's that next booking down for?'

Terry consulted the schedule. 'Some geezer at Hempnall going to Stansted at 4.45.'

'You could do that one. Standard fare,' Darren said, without irony. '£120. Enjoy that, you will.'

'Trevor's parked up at Castle Meadow,' Terry pointed out. 'His shout.'

Just at that moment they heard the heavy tread of footsteps on the stairs. Two people by the sound of it, one forging ahead, the other dallying behind. And who had we here, Terry wondered idly, only to find the corkscrew-curled head of the girl from the Iceberg bobbing up to fill the space between the stair-head and the reception-cubby-hole.

'Jan,' Darren said despairingly. 'Jan, Christ.'

There were several things to be said of this encounter. The first was that it was not a put-up job, conceived with malicious intent. You could see from the way the girl's over-lipsticked mouth opened in an 'o' like a goldfish that she had no idea she'd find Darren up this particular staircase in the Prince of Wales. The second was that, in the circumstances, Darren took it surprisingly well, just flopped down behind the desk behind the reception window and started shaking his head from side to side as if bound by invisible chains that he burned to tear off. The third was that everything would have been OK – well, more or less OK – well, manageable, anyhow – had not the owner of the second pair of footwear now clumped laboriously into view.

'Jesus, Jayce,' Jan said bitterly to this apparition, as if it was all his fault. 'Jayce. *Jesus.*'

Terry took a squint and discovered that Jason was a big lad all right, with a pair of ludicrous sideburns to boot, who looked what you might call handy. Having reached the top of the stairs at some cost to his respiratory system, he stood back on his heels, gasped for breath once or twice, looked around him, sized up the welcome party and shrugged his shoulders. Later, when they discussed the situation and its aftermath, Terry and Darren agreed that what had happened need not have happened. What would have made it not happen was Jason – Jayce – turning rapidly on his heel and heading back the way he had come. Even if he had just stood there shamefaced and humbly enquired if they could have a cab, things might not have ended the way they did. Instead, Jason removed the imploring hand that Jan had placed on the sleeve of his Crombie coat, flicked an insolent, teeth-baring grin in Darren's direction and said:

'All right, lover boy?'

For a big bloke, Darren could move with impressive speed when he wanted to. To Terry, watching with interest from behind the window, it seemed to take him only an instant to emerge into the waiting area, take Jason's legs out from under him and send him sprawling on the sofa, banging his nose on the arm-rest as he went. It was funny how those big lads always went down like tree-trunks; it was the thin, starveling rat-boys who came up game and smiling and never seemed to mind how much punishment they took. There would have been more of this – quite a lot more – had not Jan, who looked as if she had experience of this kind of scenario, had in fact spent large parts of her life breaking up fights between past and present boyfriends, flung herself dramatically between them and said with what seemed more like resignation than genuine anger: 'Just fucking leave him alone, Dazz, will you?' There wasn't much you could do after that, not here in the Abacab office in the Prince of Wales at 4 o'clock in the morning: if a woman with whom you had enjoyed intimate relations until fairly recently told you to stop doing something, then by and large you stopped doing it. Meanwhile, there was blood from Jason's nose, lots of it, going all over the sofa, and this, too, and presumably the thought of what Mr Abercrombie might say about it, served to stay Darren's hand.

'Just fucking leave him alone will you, Dazz?' Jan said,

even more wearily than the first time. 'Anyhow, he's got a weak heart.'

'He's got some fucking stupid sideburns and all,' Darren returned, giving Jason another thump for good measure.

And for what seemed an extraordinarily long period of time they stood, or in Jason's case lay, looking at each other, stricken and preoccupied, silent except for their rapidly escaping breath, while the light from the streetlamps cast huge shadows over the room and its furniture, and Terry thought of Frankie's carmined finger-nails on the car-door, and the silt-strewn carpet at the big house in Thorpe, thought, too, of all the parched Norwich faces, remembered and forgotten, and the muddy water, rising with an implacable force and urgency to sweep them effortlessly and irreclaimably away.

Agency

THE AGENCY WAS in an obscure part of town, round the back of Washington Square, not far from NYU: a picturesque neighbourhood, it had to be allowed, where the marijuana stench wafted out of the subway entrances like crop-spray and old black men went around sifting punctiliously through the garbage. When it had first moved there from plush premises in Upper Manhattan, people had complained and wondered 'what Gabby Kronstadt thought he was doing,' but these protests were disingenuous. They were disingenuous because Gabriel's prestige was such that his clients would have followed him anywhere: Great Neck; Poughkeepsie; Hell's Kitchen, even, if at the end of the journey they could have found Gabriel sitting in his curiously under-furnished office, Buddha-like and impassive, with the stack of fresh contracts on his desk and the espresso machine pulsing trails of vapour at his side. Then, after they had got over the shock of having to head down to Tenth Street, with all that entailed, Gabriel's clients began to detect advantages in the area. Someone discovered a delicatessen selling exotic bagels. Someone else turned up a friendly shoe repair store. And people would say: 'The great thing about going to see Gab these days is that you can get yourself a pastrami and apricot on the way back,' or 'That nice Mr Schulz fixed these brogues for $15.' But this, too, was disingenuous, meant to compliment Gabriel rather than expressing any satisfaction in the locale. There were other amenities which nobody ever cared to speak about, and Richard had once seen a quite successful children's writer scoring what looked like a wrap of amphetamine sulphate from a dealer stationed in the shoe repair store's doorway.

There were no dealers plying their trade this morning, although the marijuana stench was stronger than ever and the shoe repair store was closed for a Jewish holiday. Coming along the street, he was reassured by the way the sidewalk's relative anonymity suddenly yielded up a riot of familiar artefacts. There everything was again: the taped-up funeral parlour window no one had ever got round to repairing; the vegetable stalks in the gutter alongside the Ethiopian restaurant; the long red-brick expanse with the DEPOT sign hanging at a 45 degree angle; and then the Perspex-fronted vestibule with the rash of rusty brass plates on the wall beside it – the car rental firm; the pet insurers; the cut-price dentist ('Extraction with Satisfaction') and then, about two-thirds of the way down, *Kronstadt & Seltzer, Literary Agents*. There was no Mr Seltzer. He had been dead a long time.

Richard pressed the button next to the brass plate and had himself buzzed in. The vestibule's interior was nondescript but not without interest. Great things, he knew, had happened in this thousand square feet of shabby carpet and breeze-block surround. A Pulitzer Prize-winner had once tumbled down in a stupor here and been photographed by the *Post*, and the Finkelstein divorce was supposed to have kicked into gear at the foot of the staircase. Just now there was only a drift of mail over the mat and a card that said Hawaiian ladies were waiting to say Aloha, so he pressed on up the stairs, went past the door of the company that rented cheerleaders' uniforms and the mysterious portal stamped with the single word REQUISITES and came out onto a glass-caparisoned landing where, behind immense double doors, aloof and bespectacled, Mrs Keitel could be seen reading a copy of *Home and Garden*.

There were people who said that Mrs Keitel, like the bagel counter and the shoe repair store, was another of Kronstadt & Seltzer's subsidiary advantages, but this illusion was harder to sustain. She was a gaunt, grey-haired woman who had been there so long that she remembered Mr Seltzer going out to lunch with Gore Vidal and Norman Lear coming in for script conferences. The people who made a fuss about the exotic bagels or took their brogues to the shoe repair store sometimes competed to see which cinematic character she reminded them of. Just lately 'the Owl in the Parlour' had been replaced by 'one of the creatures in *Pan's Labyrinth*.' When she saw him emerge on the other side of the double doors she put down the copy of *Home and Garden*, gave a little shrug that for a moment seemed to send her whole back into spasm and said in her high, cracking voice:

'Oh, it's you is it?'

'Just got in off the plane.' You had to play it straight with Mrs K.

'Oh yeah. What's it like in England?'

'Everyone's very worried about Princess Kate.'

'I ain't interested in that Royal Family so much,' Mrs Keitel said, who had once spent five minutes cross-questioning him about the lay-out of the gardens at Sandringham. 'We got enough of our own problems over here.' Once again he was struck by how completely she dominated her environment. There were other members of staff going by – girls in Paul Smith jeans with jiffy bags under their scrawny arms, motorcycle messengers, the pale, put-upon man who tended the Royalties Department – but somehow in Mrs Keitel's presence they lost their individuality, faded away into corners, like the supporting cast in a medieval frieze, leaving Mrs Keitel to march on into the foreground, picked out in golden thread.

'How's Boromir?'

'He ain't so good, now you ask. Just last night he ate a tray of cupcakes and sicked up all over an antimacassar.'

There were people who wondered why, in a profession keen on youth and glamour, on tact, suavity and expertise, Mrs Keitel was still ruling the roost here at Kronstadt & Seltzer. But there were also people who insisted that having her there was a crucial part of Gabriel's personal myth, that if you had a legendary figure holding court in the agency's throne-room, then you needed an equally legendary figure guarding its drawbridge, that Gab and Mrs Keitel, however sharply differentiated or temperamentally opposed, were made for each other. If there was a flaw in this argument, it might have been that Mrs Keitel seemed unaware of the role she was expected to play.

The phone rang a couple of times and then went dead. Mrs Keitel looked at it suspiciously and then clawed at the side of her head as if she was trying to dislodge something caught up in her tangled hair. 'Don't get so many calls these days,' she pronounced. 'Don't get so many people coming in, neither. All on account of the pandemic. Hey,' she said. 'You ever write poetry?'

This was unprecedented. In all the times he had stood in the reception area Mrs Keitel had never once asked him what he wrote. She was famous for taking no interest at all in anything anyone represented by Kronstadt & Seltzer got up to professionally.

'Sometimes. Do you?'

'I been writing some a little,' Mrs Keitel conceded. 'Sonnets, mostly. Find it difficult to stick to a rhyme-scheme, though. Kind of gets out of hand.' And then suddenly the light that had come into her eye at the mention of poetry faded away and she gave a little zestless pout.

'Hey, you better go see Gab. He said he was expecting you.'

There were strange hieroglyphs scrawled over the shiny cover of *Home and Garden*, and next to the photograph of somebody's New England rockery a single sentence written in inch-high capitals: *And I a twister love what I abhor.*

'I hope Boromir's feeling better.'

Just as Mrs Keitel's shadow hung over the reception area, instantly reducing anyone else who walked into it to the status of cipher, so the corridor that led out of it into the inner recesses of the building was dominated by Gabriel. The wall was full of photographs of distinguished Kronstadt & Seltzer authors, but somehow the effect of this tableau was to make them seem less celebrated, darkly aware that the trail of their distinction went back to the

man who sat at the corridor's end. Inspecting the picture
of a woman whose second and third novels Gabriel was
supposed to have sold to Houghton Mifflin for three-quarters of a million dollars, Richard realised that she seemed
not so much cast down as hangdog, as if she suspected
that at bottom her success was arbitrary, that Gabriel had
simply used her as a vehicle for the exercise of his will,
that dozens of other people were equally deserving of the
three-quarters of a million dollars advance, the visiting
professorship at Duke and the reconditioned farmhouse
in Connecticut.

Toc, toc, toc. Tikka, tikka, tikka. Another thing about
the building was the weird, non-human soundtrack that
pulsed around its passageways. Just now a whole posse of
goblins were clearly marauding their way back to Moria
through the cavity wall insulation. The pipes in the gentleman's bathroom burped and hissed like the static-heavy
German electronica albums he had collected in teendom.
Two-thirds of the way along the corridor that led to
Gabriel's office the photos of Kronstadt & Seltzer's celebrity
authors gave out and were replaced by pictures of Gabriel
himself: Gabriel with Hilary Clinton; Gabriel showing a
badly-flummoxed Henry Kissinger where to sign his name
on a contract; Gabriel staring blandly at a moustachioed
man who, memory insisted, had once played bass in the
Eagles; each one of them chastened and suborned by their
exposure to the paralysing force of Gabriel's will. Gabriel
photographed badly; or rather portraits of him gave no
idea of what lurked beneath his apparently meek exterior.
The camera took his intransigence and made it seem half-
way benign. And looking at the figure who now loomed

into view through his office window, Richard decided that it missed something else as well: the oddly submerged quality, as if Gab had just emerged from a longish spell underwater.

Tikka, tikka, slicka. The noises were fading away now, turning dim. Perhaps the goblins had gone off to sack Rivendell. Gabriel had a telephone – one of the three that sat on his desk -clamped to his right ear, so firmly that it looked as if it might be stuck there with adhesive, but he saw Richard through the glass and beckoned him in. The final stretches of Gabriel's phone calls were always worth listening to. This time Richard was pretty sure he heard the words *every last copy taken out of the warehouse and burnt.* Whoever was at the other end must have objected to this, as Gabriel unhooked the receiver from his ear, looked at it as if he had never seen one before and wondered to what uses it might be put, said 'Yes, no, *of course,*' in a brisk tone and then put the phone down.

And I a twister love what I abhor. 'One thing you have to remember,' an old man with white hair had told him at a Kronstadt & Seltzer authors' party twenty years before, 'is that Gab just *loves* us. All of us. Each and every one.' Richard had wondered about this, about its implications and the collateral suspicions it pushed into view – whether in the end there was anyone in the world whom Gabriel could be said to regard in this promising light. There was a Mrs Gab back home in Coney Island and a son who worked in a brokerage on Fifty-third. What did Gab think of them? In the meantime, Gab's office looked exactly as it always had done: sparse, unornamented, more like an anchorite's cell than a literary agent's parlour. The

blown-up facsimile of the *New Yorker* profile in which Gab
had suggested that the managing director of Farrar, Straus
& Giroux wasn't fit to run a burger joint on the East River
and remarked, of Erica Jong, that he 'had enough of these
boss chicks' was still framed under glass on the wall above
his head, but there were one or two more books with titles
like *Manacling the Muse: Tax and the Entertainment Industry*
and the espresso machine had disappeared.

'You want coffee?' Gabriel said, without preamble. His
voice was oddly husky, not exactly menacing but conscious
of the effect it produced. Not waiting for a reply, he picked
up the phone again and buzzed reception. 'Two coffees,
Myrtle . . . Hey,' he went on. 'You notice anything weird
about Mrs K?'

Unlike the *New Yorker* profile and the little pile of
books, this was a departure. Gab never took any interest in
his worker ants. Richard wondered whether he had noticed
anything weird about Mrs Keitel. It depended how you
defined weird, and what you thought about the people,
all of them by definition larger than life, who worked
for New York literary agencies. He decided to stick to
the facts.

'She asked me if I wrote poetry. There was a piece of
paper on the desk with a line from Empson on it.'

'Yeah?' There was no way of knowing whether Gabriel
regarded the Empson quote as a point in Mrs Keitel's
favour. 'Well it makes a change from those property magazines she's always leaving around the place. Not that that
walk-up in Yonkers she has couldn't do with a refit.'

There was no sign of the coffee. Becalmed on the client's
side of Gabriel's pool table-sized roll-top, Richard became

aware that another vital part of Kronstadt & Seltzer's
atmospheric jigsaw had clicked silently into place. This was
its unreality. The light of the desk-lamp shining off the top
of Gab's bald head and the wispy beard-stalks sprouting
underneath made him look like the king of the goblin
band who marauded through the cavity wall insulation.
Outside the window there was tumult in the late-after-
noon sky, little flashes of colour and sparking lights, as if
half-a-dozen alien spacecraft were about to come down on
Washington Square.

'How's business?'

'*Bizniz*?' Gabriel rolled the word around his tongue,
altogether mystified, as if he had never heard it before. 'It's
not so good. None of these young agents have any respect.'
As a young agent, Gab had been famous for not having any
respect. 'And then half the people who write books these
days are illiterate. But we'll do OK with Joey Alessandro's
memoir, I reckon.'

Richard couldn't remember if Joey Alessandro was
the mob boss or the celebrity chef who had poisoned
his wife. Very quietly, which was a sign of his serious
displeasure, Gabriel repeated the coffee order into the
microphone. Outside the air was turning blue-grey.
Down in Washington Square the crazy people would be
smoking inflammable substances and crashing around on
skateboards or seeing if they could march into the hotels
without being stopped by the doormen It was sometime
since Richard had written one of his Sunday newspaper
articles about the vibrancy of New York life. Thinking
about this neglect of a fail-safe revenue-stream, he realised
that it was one of those articles that had propelled him

into Gabriel's clutches in the first place. *Forty-second Street isn't Forty-fourth Street*, Gab had cryptically remarked, in the act of inviting him to be represented by Kronstadt & Seltzer, *and neither is it Forty-third*. Just now Gabriel had extracted a slim blue folder from the pile on his desk and was pressing it gratefully against his torso as if it was some kind of newfangled stab-vest.

'I think I can work with *Unburnt Boats*,' he said, after a while. 'You want me to talk you through it?'

There was always something vaguely terrifying about the way Gabriel went about transacting business, a bit like the manner in which an invading general might invest an enemy city: disposing his troops; stopping up exits and entrances; devising bold strokes; picking up provender; giving no quarter. Within a couple of minutes Richad had heard exactly how much money he was likely to be paid for *Unburnt Boats*, who was going to pay it to him and when he could expect to get it. He tried a question about Polish rights, but it was no good: Gabriel had the email from the sub-agent out of the file almost before he had begun to speak. As well as being faintly terrifying, there was also something vaguely dispiriting about this process: chance; nuance; possibility – none of these got a look-in when ranged against Gabriel's rapt, inflexible gaze. If he said you were going to earn a hundred thousand dollars, you would earn a hundred thousand dollars. If he said your career was washed up, your career was washed up. It was as simple as that.

'. . . Twoj Styl will publish the August after next and there's a clause in the contract tying the translation to a January deadline date,' Gabriel said, coming to the end of his summary of the situation in Warsaw. A noise in the corridor that had woven its way in and out of the last couple of sentences was growing louder and they looked up to see what it was. Mrs Keitel, though squarely in the line of vision, gave no sign of having noticed them, but continued to do whatever it was she was doing, an activity that involved wearing her raincoat indoors and keeping both her arms pressed tightly to her sides.

'What the hell is that woman up to?' Gabriel wondered. He could sometimes be nervous with underlings, not quite sure how best to suborn them. 'Is she coming in here? The fuck does she want?'

Time, which had slowed down while Gabriel was discussing the Polish rights, began to quicken up again. One of the secretaries came hastening along the corridor, stopped to say a word to Mrs Keitel and got something back that made her spring away as if she had been stung in the ear. Outside the window a helicopter came barrelling into view so rapidly that it looked as if it were about to collide with the top of the Kronstadt & Seltzer building, only to sheer away at the very last moment. Richard thought about all the other literary agents in whose offices he had sat: airy, expansive women with outsize spectacles; playful men in red braces; blushing girls out of whom all the arty nonsense had yet to be knocked. He had a feeling that compared to Gabriel, they were all lacking some vital ingredient, some essential piece of knowledge about the way the world worked.

Mrs Keitel was inside the doorway now, the downward slant of her arms explained by the fact that she was dragging two outsize carrier bags overloaded with office supplies. Richard thought that in the quarter of an hour since he had last set eyes on her something had gone seriously wrong, that she looked greyer and sadder but somehow more determined, decisive, sure of herself. There was a big snowstorm paperweight on the corner of Gabriel's desk, enclosing a view of the uptown skyscrapers, and she picked it up, shook it furiously and inspected the cascade of artificial snowflakes with grim satisfaction.

The bags full of office supplies – there were half-a-dozen gunmetal staplers sticking out of the one next to Richard's feet – and the snowstorm-shaking were too big to be ignored. 'What seems to be the trouble, Myrtle?' Gabriel gravely enquired. The paperweight fell on the floor and broke apart, whether by accident or design no one quite knew. In the silence that followed its descent, Gabriel tried again:

'What exactly are you up to, Myrtle? I mean, are you OK?'

'You know what?' Mrs Keitel said, about three times louder than the size of the room required. 'I quit. That's what I've come here for. To tell you that I'm quitting.'

Richard could tell that Gabriel was upset by the smashed paperweight. He got up from his chair, bent down and began to pick one or two of the larger fragments out of the carpet. A shard of glass stuck momentarily to the tip of his finger and he stared stoically at the spot of blood it left behind.

'Don't worry about that,' Gabriel said, waving him back to his seat. 'You've been with us a long time, Myrtle. Why do you want to leave?'

'You'd quit if you were me,' Mrs Keitel said, quite

mildly, as if it were a philosophical point that needed arguing out. Then her tone changed. 'You know what?' She was talking to Richard now. 'He's an asshole. He is, though. You know what he did once, back in the day? He was doing a deal with some stiff at Knopf. Three-volume history of the Korean War or some such. And he sent a fax – you remember faxes? – a hand-written fax, saying he wanted $300,000. The guy misreads the '3' as a '5' and faxes back to say, yeah, half-a-million dollars is fine. And Gab here, he doesn't say anything. Just takes the money and buys himself a new station wagon.'

'Myrtle . . .' Gabriel said, but Mrs Keitel ignored him. In her excitement, she half-upset one of the carrier bags, allowing several reels of parcel-tape to fall out of it.

'Yeah, we had an affair once,' she went on. 'You know, just one of those after-hours things. Hanging around in dive-bars. Hotels up in the Sixties. And do you know what he used to call his doodle? I'll tell you. *The one-eyed snake in the turtle-neck.*

'Myrtle . . .' Gabriel said again.

'And another thing,' Mrs Keitel announced, swivelling on one of her large, moccasin-shod feet and throwing out a fat hand to secure another reel of parcel-tape that threatened to escape, '*I voted for Trump.*'

In the doorway, where the equally-distributed weight of the bags reduced her to a kind of bobbing equilibrium, her eye fell on Richard. 'You're OK,' she said, and then to Gabriel, in what could have been intended as an ironic reproach or a simple statement of fact: 'He asked after my cat.' And then she was gone, leaving the remaining fragments of the snowstorm paperweight trodden into the carpet and two abandoned staplers lodged against the door-frame.

A terrible, accusatory silence fell over the room. Outside the twilight had begun to fill up the gaps between the buildings. They could hear Mrs Keitel racketing back to reception. A succession of small thuds suggested that she was discarding the stationery supplies as she went. All this continued for several minutes. In the end Gabriel said in a subdued way:

'It simply isn't true about the Knopf deal. I'll admit I made a lot of money out of it, but not at all in the way she says. And I never said anything about a one-eyed snake in a turtle-neck.'

'She seemed very upset.'

'Yes, she was, wasn't she?' Gabriel said, as if being upset was a concept that he had only just been introduced to and wondered whether it would catch on. He was silent again for a moment or two and then opened his mouth with a jolt.

'That paperweight was a present from Tom Wolfe.'

Arriving back in reception five minutes later, Richard discovered that Mrs Keitel had left a trail of destruction in her wake. A coffee percolator and three or four cups had been thrown on the floor, several of the telephones had had their wires pulled out of the wall and the fire alarm had been switched on. A couple of Gabriel's junior assistants were quietly clearing up the mess, as if to emphasize by their lack of self-consciousness what dramatic and star-crossed lives they also led.

'Was Mrs Keitel OK?'

'She didn't exactly say,' one of the women returned.

'Took about five hundred dollars' worth of office supplies with her, though.'

Down in the vestibule another drift of circulars had arrived on the mat from creative realtors, plasterers, pizza-sellers and girls who were new in town. He swept them aside with the toe of his shoe and stepped out into the street, which as ever was full of piles of tin cans. There was no one about and the bagel counter where you could buy such startling combinations of sweet and sour had its double doors padlocked together. *And I a twister love what I abhor.* He decided that he could either go back to his hotel or head up to the Lotos Club to attend a cocktail party given by a friend who wanted to introduce everyone to his new Bulgarian wife. There was a figure marching down the sidewalk towards him – no more than a shape at this distance – and he watched it loom into view, gradually separate itself from the black plastic sacks and the piled-up debris and turn into Mrs Keitel. She was moving fast and had got rid of the carrier bags somewhere; her moccasins made slapping noises on the asphalt. For a moment he thought that she was about to stop and talk to him – he would have liked to hear more about the Knopf deal, about Gabriel, life in Yonkers, even Boromir and his cupcake orgy – but with the minimum of eye contact Mrs Keitel, like some human quinquereme, sailed effortlessly on. In the days to come, people would have all kinds of things to say about Mrs Keitel's defection. All manner of mythological imaginings would be projected above her gaunt, grey head. And he suspected that most of them would be wrong, or misguided, or mischievous, and that it was his duty to resist these patterns and behavioural mosaics and ensure that Mrs Keitel should be remembered not as a symbol of some gathering crisis in the affairs of Kronstadt & Seltzer, but merely as herself. But for the moment he contented himself with watching her pass by, her face suffused with a mysterious power and calm that had not been there before, off and away into the city's dark yet welcoming heart.

Out of Season

Towards the middle of September the hotel showed signs of closing down. There was a paradox about this procedure, as the immediate consequence was that everything seemed suddenly busy – even busier than it had been at the summer's height. The telephone rang more often at the reception desk; there was more luggage piled up in the vestibule and more taxis coming from Toulon to fetch it; and Hannah, sneaking into the billiards room early one morning, had found it full of stacked cabin trunks awaiting despatch. On the other hand, proof of changing circumstance was evident in the diminishing number of guests who could be seen eating in the restaurant. Every day and at every meal another two or three of them seemed to have slipped away. The Italian businessmen and the women who were not their wives went back to Turin. The pair of pig-tailed Scottish girls who had spent the summer eating *glace de framboise* at the novelty store on the esplanade or playing halma in the residents' lounge were returned to their boarding school. The artistic English gentleman who had wandered around the beach trying to find a spot to set up his easel disappeared to Marseille. Everywhere

Hannah looked, the clock seemed to be winding down: the continental edition of the *Daily Mail*, with its headlines about Signor Mussolini and Herr von Ribbentrop stopped arriving with the morning post; the sea turned grey and fretful, and the fishing boats lay drawn up in a row on the shale. If there was any consolation, it lay in the fact that Mutti – this was not always the case – remained cheerful. On the night when there were only five people apart from themselves at dinner in the restaurant she explained that, no, the hotel was not really closing down – no proper hotel ever really closed – but would, in fact, remain open for the benefit of its permanent guests.

As for the winter months that lay ahead, the best plan, Mutti explained, was to avoid idleness and to keep one's spirits up. On hearing these instructions, Hannah, Ilsa and Hedwig looked cautiously at each other. They had been advised to keep their spirits up so often that the exhortation had no meaning. The best way to avoid idleness, Mutti continued, was to make a schedule: in this way each day might be conveniently arranged to offer something that they could look forward to. On hearing this, the girls looked at each other again: they were used to schedules and rosters and diaries in which great stretches of time were broken up by trivial appointments. 'What shall we do?' Ilsa asked, who of the three of them was the one who most often tried to curry favour with Mutti. And so, as the long evening declined, and the lamps were lit on the veranda, and the solitary waiter glided back and forth across the room like a grey ghost, they sat and plotted how they might endure a winter in Sanary-sur-Mer with the tourists gone and the amusement parlour shut and the row of cottages behind the dunes locked up and deserted. Certain of these engagements were already set in stone. On Monday mornings, for example, they went to French conversation with Mme Carpentier, and on Wednesday afternoons they attended Mass at the Catholic church. But there were other things, Mutti suggested, that they could do in addition to their studies. They could, for example, take one of the buses that plied the coast road to Toulon and inspect the ancient fort. They could, for example, visit the sisters at the convent. They could, for example, keep a scrapbook of their activities in Sanary-sur-Mer and beyond in which their father would be interested. The girls nodded their heads at these suggestions, but privately they were sceptical about the scrapbook. At last even the solitary waiter went away and they sat in near-darkness until the clock struck ten.

All this happened on a Sunday. On the Monday morning the last of the cabin trunks had disappeared from the billiard room and they walked down to the Place de la Concorde for their lesson with Mme Carpentier. Mme Carpentier was a middle-aged lady with legs so large and misshapen that they looked like giant vegetable stalks; she spoke questionable French and said things like *En silence, mes élèves* and *Charles Dickens était un écrivain anglais distingué.* On this particular morning, once they had eaten the madeleine biscuits that Mme Carpentier customarily set out and drunk glasses of a brown liquid that Mme Carpentier assured them was Coca-Cola, she asked them their ages.

'J'ai dix ans,' Hedwig said.

'J'ai douze ans,' Ilsa said.

'J'ai quinze ans,' Hannah said, which was not strictly

accurate as her birthday was not until November. Then, rather unnecessarily, she asked: 'Et quelle nombre des ans avait vouz, madame?' And Mme Carpentier said: 'C'est une affaire privée.'

When, at the end of the lesson, which was as tedious as ever, Hannah gave Mme Carpentier the white envelope that Mutti had entrusted to her as they stood in the vestibule of the hotel doing up their mackintoshes, she said: 'There is a discrepancy. A mistake. Will you tell your mother that next week she should send the extra ten francs?' Hannah said that she would do this. 'And give your mother my affectionate good wishes,' Mme Carpentier added, not wholly sincerely.

After the lesson they walked back to the hotel through fine autumn rain, inspected the window of the butcher's shop, which was empty except for an enormous pig's head, and held a skipping match on the cobbled stones. Through all this time Hannah thought about her sisters and about the sisters in the children's books she had read when she was younger, who lived in *Schlossen* in Bavaria or went to exotic boarding schools, had vivid personalities, talked in code and enjoyed a constant stream of adventures involving runaway trains and snowstorms and animals that had escaped from the circus. But it was impossible to fit Ilsa and Hedwig into these patterns. They were demure, unassuming girls who liked embroidery and jigsaw puzzles and would have fainted with dismay had they met an animal that had escaped from the circus, whereas the sisters in the children's books were skilled at constructing concealed traps or summoning doughty foresters to haul them back into captivity. All this, as she acknowledged, was very disappointing, although as she well knew (the children's books had had something to say about this) it was there to be borne. If there was one quality that distinguished the fictional sisters, it was that they did not complain. Their parents might be kidnapped by pirates while on restorative voyages around the Caribbean; their family fortunes might be mysteriously embezzled, forcing them to live with undesirable relatives; they were sometimes subjected to debilitating illnesses and lay pale and subdued in sick rooms for months on end; but they did not repine, and stoicism saw them through.

Back at the hotel they discovered that in their absence a new guest had arrived. He was an Englishman, red-haired and his middle thirties, with a surprisingly small amount of luggage who, when they came into the lounge, was sitting at a table with Mutti drinking coffee. 'This is Mr Tozer,' Mutti said, not quite cordially. 'You may say good morning to him.' And so all the girls said, 'Good morning, Mr Tozer,' and gave respectful bobs of their heads. If Mutti had said that Mr Tozer was the Graf von Hollenherzen they would have given little curtsies. And Mr Tozer said 'Yes indeed,' a bit abstractedly, as if his mind were elsewhere. The wind was getting up and their conversation with him was interrupted by people looking out of the window in the direction of the wild waves. In the course of the next few days they saw quite a lot of Mr Tozer. He came to dinner and said 'Good evening' rather too many times. When the weather allowed, he sat on the veranda reading or making notes in a grey exercise book. Once, when they encountered him in this way, Mutti, whose attitude to Mr Tozer seemed to have thawed, said 'Mr Tozer is an author. Perhaps, if you are lucky, he will put you in one of his books.' And the three of them said dutifully, 'Thank you Mr Tozer,' and Mr Tozer said, 'What very polite girls,' and got a wry smile from Mutti, who did not like her children to be complimented in public. After dinner, when she and Mr Tozer had taken a turn at bezique in the lounge, she said, 'I am not sure Mr Tozer is *gemütlich*. But he is certainly a gentleman. And when one is thrown on one's own resources, it is sometimes necessary to make allowances.'

It turned out that Mutti, though she had yet to make up her mind about Mr Tozer, had been serious about the scrapbook. She bought a large, cardboard-covered volume with coloured pages from the stationers in the town, and each evening the girls were required to sit at a table in the lounge adding material to it. There was some doubt as to what might be suitable, but Ilsa and Hedwig decided to paste in picture postcards and a copy of the dinner menu with asterisks next to the dishes they had eaten. Hannah, thinking this approach unimaginative and juvenile, wrote a diary so that their father would have some idea of their activities in Sanary-sur-Mer. *Today we went for a walk along the beach*, she wrote. *It was quite cold and Mutti made us wear scarves.* The next day she wrote: *We went for lessons at Mme Carpentier's. We sang* 'Frère Jacques' *and* 'Sur le pont d'Avignon.' What she did not write was that Mme Carpentier, who seemed unusually cross, had sent another message to Mutti about the missing ten francs. Mutti approved of their efforts. She said: 'Your father will be interested to see this. He will like to know that his girls have been busy.' Sometimes in the morning they would find a letter addressed to their mother pinned to the big green-baize board in the vestibule, and Mutti would say things like: 'Your father has gone to see those film people in Munich,' or 'Your father has gone to Marienbad to take the waters for his health. He sends his best love.' 'Will Father write to us soon?' Hannah asked on one of these occasions, and Mutti said that their father was very busy but would assuredly write to them all and would certainly not forget Hannah's birthday in November.

It was getting on into October now. The number of residents, including themselves and Mr Tozer, had dwindled to eight, and one of those was an old lady with asthma who never left her room. An entire floor of the hotel had been closed down, and the furniture in the billiard room had been covered in dust-sheets. The menu, too, became more limited and there was a depressing evening when they dined on *bouillon* and *loups de mer*. Still Mutti tried to keep their spirits up. It was highly possible that their father would send for them before Christmas, she explained; failing that, they could go and stay with their relatives in Wurttemberg. Mr Tozer had taken to dining at the same table as them. He sent back the *loups de mer* untouched, but continued to say 'Good evening' whenever anyone looked his way. That evening, just as they were finishing the watery *crème brûlée* which made do as a dessert, M. Delavacquerie, the hotel manager, came into the room, bowed, and whispered something in Mutti's ear which caused her to stiffen slightly in her chair, give M. Delavacquerie a nod and say, 'In a very short time, I assure you,' before he backed humbly away.

The girls shared a bedroom two doors down from Mutti. There were maps on the wall of the South of

France and the Mediterranean, and also, for some reason, of Australia. That night, when Mutti had extinguished the lamp and gone back to her own room, they switched it on again, crowded into Isla's bed and discussed who, in the fullness of time, they might marry.

Hedwig said that she would marry Herr von Ribbentrop, because he looked a kind man, and the others laughed and said: anyhow, he is married already and what would Frau von Ribbentrop say?

Ilsa said that she would marry a baker and serve behind the counter in his shop, but that it would be an exclusive establishment and Jewish people would not be admitted, and they nodded their heads at the reasonableness of this.

Hannah said that she would not marry anyone, but that she wished to be a nun and live in a convent, like their great-aunt Trudl, and devote her life to prayer. This was not in the least true, but it was worth it for the awed expressions that appeared on Ilsa and Hedwig's faces.

In the morning the old lady who suffered from asthma was so ill that a doctor had to be summoned. He was an elderly man who had treated the children for sore throats in the summer, and Mutti had praised his medical skill. Although there was some mild excitement in the sight of the doctor's black bag and the stethoscope which hung round his neck as he spoke gravely to M. Delavacquerie in the vestibule, all the time Hannah found herself thinking of the girls in the children's stories she had read. The girls were, above all, resourceful. They made the best of bad situations. Their parents might have been kidnapped by pirates, or been bankrupted by designing business associates, but they never lost hope and took steps to repair their misfortunes. In this spirit, when they had eaten lunch and Ilsa and Hedwig had gone to the bedroom for their afternoon nap, a routine from which Hannah was now excused, she said to Mutti:

'May I be allowed to go for a walk?'

Mutti was not so much surprised as amused. 'Where would you like to walk?'

'I should like to walk along the beach,' Hannah said, who had not really thought about possible destinations.

'You must remember your raincoat,' Mutti said. 'And be back within the hour. Is that understood?'

It was understood, and she put on her mackintosh and made her way the short distance along the esplanade, down the big wooden steps, where moss was starting to grow in the crevices, and onto the sand. There was no one about except for a man walking in the distance who might have been Mr Tozer, and when she set off in the opposite direction she had the place to herself. The sand soon gave out and she found herself in a landscape made up of shingle, the foothills of the dunes and an occasional upturned fishing boat. A long way ahead of her there were dogs running erratically back and forth. The shingle sloped dramatically and magnified the crash of the waves, and she stopped and threw a flat stone horizontally into one of the gaps, but it was too rough for skimming stones. There were white birds flying around and she looked at them for a while with her hands plunged into the depths of her pocket, white birds that were buffeted by the wind but found ingenious ways of darting beneath the currents and resuming their flight. This cheered her up, because it spoke of resourcefulness, of being able to circumvent obstacles, of not being thrown off course by barriers that were placed in your way. In this spirit she veered right into the first outcrop of dunes, where it was easier to take shelter from the rain, stamping her feet up and down and thinking that it was not fair that girls had to wear skirts in such circumstances. On the other hand, she had a cousin who was sometimes made to wear *lederhosen* even in winter, so it struck her that there were worse things to be sent out in. She found a packet of sweets in one of her pockets – not many, but enough to occupy her for five minutes – and she wondered if there was anywhere she might sit down and eat them. There was a hut nestling beneath two of the dunes which had seen better days, and she marched up to it, noted the cracked window and the half-open door, and, after a moment of hesitation, stepped inside.

The hut was more promising than its exterior had suggested. The walls had been lined with tar paper and there was a convex mirror hanging askew on one of them with a picture postcard of Claudette Colbert stuck into the frame, and she admired the way Mlle Colbert had plucked her eyebrows and the elegant pallor of her face. The floor was less inviting, as one or two of the timbers had rotted and there were things scuttling underneath, but she leaned against the wall next to the mirror, which was spotted with tiny flecks of rust, and ate her sweets, grateful to have found shelter and, as she supposed, to be out of the reach of the world, away from Mutti and Ilsa and Hedwig and the necessity to sit in the hotel lounge playing board games or exclaiming at the noise of the sea. On the way in she had seen a piece of discarded carpet which, after who knew what adventures, had come to rest a few feet from the door and, on impulse, she stepped out onto the sand, retrieved it and laid it out in the centre of the floor. The effect was pleasing rather than the reverse, and she wondered what else she could do to improve the hut. Then, inspecting her watch, she discovered that only twenty minutes of the hour allotted to her remained and it was time to be getting back. But she was relieved to find that the faint air of gloom with which she had begun the afternoon had lifted. She was pleased with her resource-fulness. It was something the girls in the children's stories might have done.

The spirit of mild exhilaration which she took with her back to the hotel turned out to come in handy, as it enabled her to survive the two serious disturbances of the next forty-eight hours. The first came when they arrived at Mme Carpentier's to find that she was even crosser than usual. That morning they did not sing 'Frère Jacques' or 'Sur le Pont d'Avignon', but had to sit and listen while Mme Carpentier read them an unappetising story about a small boy who was attacked by a bull after disobeying instruc-tions not to stray into a farmer's field but was restored to health after his pious sister prayed for his recovery. The story was so boring that Hannah spent the half-hour which it occupied wondering how she might redecorate the inte-rior of the hut and whether it would be possible to abstract certain items from the hotel without anybody noticing. Then, at the end of the lesson, Mme Carpentier said that it was most unfortunate but owing to certain irregulari-ties, of which their mother was aware, the lessons would have to be discontinued. The second disturbance came that evening when, having brushed off Mme Carpentier's remarks on the grounds that she was a foolish woman who would be better off working in a shop, Mutti announced that she had decided to travel to Munich, where certain matters demanded her attention, and would be gone a week. Seeing the looks of alarm on the girls' faces, she softened her expression, which had previously been merely businesslike, and said that everything had been arranged, that Mme Delavacquerie would keep an eye on them and that Mme Coubertin had kindly offered to superintend their lessons. Mme Coubertin was an elderly widow who lived in the hotel *en permanence* and whom nobody liked on account of her excitable Pomeranian and her habit of asking the waiter to carry small parcels for her which she could perfectly well have carried herself, but the children, seeing what was expected of them, said that they would do their best.

'Will you be seeing Daddy?' Ilsa asked, who could think of no other reason why their mother should be going to Munich. And Mutti said that, yes, she probably would. And Hedwig asked if she would be taking the scrapbook to show him, at which Mutti said no, she thought the scrapbook could wait until another time. Two days later she was gone, and the girls spent their time sitting in the lounge while Mme Coubertin read to them from books that were even more boring than Mme Carpentier's, being fussed over by Mme Delavacquerie, who insisted that they eat milk pudding with their tea, and listening to the sound of the waves crashing on the beach.

On the second evening, after the others had gone to sleep, Hannah put on her best frock, smoothed her hair back carefully from her forehead, went down to the restaurant and sat at one of the tables. There was hardly anyone about, although Mr Tozer could be seen in the far corner reading a book by the light of a spirit-lamp. When Albert the waiter came across to see what she wanted she said: 'Could I have the dinner menu, please?' She was half-afraid that Albert would point out that she had already eaten her tea in the housekeeper's room, and that Mutti had not said anything about evening meals, but he merely nodded, said, 'Yes, mademoiselle,' and brought her an oblong slip of yellow paper. There was not very much on the menu, but she decided on a bowl of soup and some chicken breast. Then, after she had ordered this, greatly daring, she said: 'And I could I possibly have a glass of white wine? Hock, if you have it.' She had once heard her father say that civilised people drank hock and that sauternes were for washing your automobile with. And Albert went to kitchen and returned with a glass of hock. She drank the wine in neat, dainty sips, ate the soup and about two-thirds of the chicken, which came in a nasty pink sauce, and then went back to her room feeling that in some obscure way she had proved a point.

The next day it rained and Mme Coubertin, declaring herself *souffrante*, was not available to superintend their lessons, so they sat in the lounge kicking their legs against the furniture and reading a two-day-old copy of the *Nice Matin* which had somehow fetched up there. Hannah thought that she was growing tired of Ilsa and Hedwig, who did not wish to talk about interesting things and had limited horizons. In the afternoon, without explanation, and taking with her a small footstool concealed under her mackintosh, she went down to the beach again and made her way to the dunes. Here everything was just as she had left it, although the picture-postcard of Claudette Colbert was turning spongy from the damp, so she placed the footstool advantageously in the centre of the carpet, squatted on it and began to consider other refinements that she might profitably introduce. 'Where have you been, Hannah?' Ilsa asked when she returned to the hotel, and she said: 'For a walk. Why, where have you been?' And Ilsa and Hedwig, who knew that Hannah was cross about something, said that they had been playing snakes and ladders in the lounge.

That evening Hannah put on her best frock again, went down to the restaurant, examined the menu card, which was even sparser than on the previous night, and ordered a veal escalope and some haricot beans. There was nobody in the room except Mr Tozer, who was dining frugally off an omelette, a peach and a bottle of Vichy water. After a bit he left his seat, came over to her table and placed a magazine on the cloth next to her plate.

'I wonder if this would interest you?' he said. 'There is a poem of mine in it. Not a very good poem, but a poem nonetheless. The magazine was called the *New English Weekly*, and in truth did not look very interesting. All the same, she thanked Mr Tozer and went back to her veal escalope. He was better looking than he had first seemed, she thought, and his red hair was less offensive. Also, he was wearing a pink-and-white jacket with gold braid on the cuffs which she knew must have cost a considerable amount of money. The poem, which she read later that night in her room, was about a woman called Louise who had 'designing breasts' and was what Mutti would have called 'warm.' Nonetheless, she read it with interest because this was the first time she had ever met someone who had written anything beyond a business memorandum, a diary or – in Mutti's case – long letters to obscure relatives in Ruthenia.

It was getting on to the end of October now, and although Mutti had been gone for several days the children were not especially concerned by her absence. This had happened before, and they appreciated the comparative room for manoeuvre that it allowed them. Making use of these opportunities, Ilsa and Hedwig ordered poached eggs for breakfast rather than the toast and jam to which they were accustomed and made surreptitious jokes about Mme Delavacquerie's over-enthusiastic use of face-powder, while Hannah looked loftily on. She had schemes of her own in prospect, one of which was the continued refurbishment of the hut. The footstool and the piece of carpet were not enough. That afternoon while the others were curled up in armchairs in the lounge she stole into the deserted kitchen and purloined a pair of willow-pattern teacups, hid one in each pocket of her mackintosh and slipped out onto the beach. The wind was blowing in off the sea and even the birds were having trouble forging a path through the currents, but by keeping her head down and winding her scarf around her face she managed to get to the hut without difficulty. Once again, everything was as she had left it, except that there was a dead crab lying on one of the rotting floor-boards. She brought out the two teacups and set them down on the square of carpet. She had been worried that they might look incongruous, but there was something satisfying about their presence in the hut, with the wind coming in through the cracks in the tar-paper and the gulls skirling overhead. She wondered what Mutti would say if she knew about the hut and she decided that it was important that Mutti, not to mention Ilsa and Hedwig, should be kept in ignorance. There was precedence for this in the children's stories, for if the girls in them had been friendly and solicitous and bent on collective action, then they had also, on occasion, been calculating and secretive, had, for example, crept out at night to bury things in the garden of the *Schloss* where they were quartered, or attempted to discover items that had themselves been buried there years before, and all this without in the least disarranging their hair or getting mud on their nightdresses, whereas her own hair, when she returned to the hotel, was so blown about by the wind that she had to spend several minutes in the vestibule coaxing it back into place.

The girls were still sitting in the lounge. Rather to her disappointment, they did not seem interested in where she had been. As she came in, Ilsa said:

'Surely Mutti will be back from Munich soon. It is eight days now and she said it would only be a week.'

'She will be back when she is back,' Hannah said. She had discovered, slightly to her surprise, that she was not at all concerned by Mutti's absence. Somebody would have to look after them. It was as simple as that. If necessary their father could be summoned to fetch them. This, too, had happened before.

'Do you think M. Delavacquerie will know how to get in touch with her?' Hedwig asked.

'No, I don't,' Hannah said. 'He is a hotel-owner. How would he know where Mutti is? You must not be so foolish.'

Nonetheless, by the time she went to bed after eating another veal escalope in the restaurant, Hannah had decided that Mutti's absence was concerning, and if it lasted another forty-eight hours it would become a serious matter. The next morning it started raining well before dawn – they could hear the raindrops rattling on the roof – and Mme Delavacquerie was so out of sorts that she could hardly bring herself to speak to them. And then, quite unexpectedly, there was the sound of a taxi drawing up outside the hotel and Albert, who happened to be in the vestibule, was helping Mutti with her suitcase. When she had put the suitcase down and shaken the water off her raincoat the girls clustered round her and asked: what had it been like in Munich, and had she seen their father? And Mutti said that it had been very cold in Munich, and unfortunately she had not seen him, but she had spoken to him on the telephone and he sent his best love. And Hannah decided that Mutti, for all the glamour of her silk stockings and marcelled hair and the Rexine suitcase with A von R in gilt letters next to the handle, was a poor fish and could have contrived some way of seeing their father, or at least pretended that she had done so.

After that life at the hotel settled down again. Mutti did not seem to mind the extra charges on the restaurant bill. The only obvious change to their previous circumstances was that two little English boys in the care of their nurse arrived one afternoon in a private car from Marseille and were installed in a bedroom on the upper floor. And yet the girls were conscious that certain things were not as they had been. One of these things was that their French lessons with Mme Carpentier mysteriously resumed. Sadly,

in the interval between their last lesson, the girls had lost
whatever respect they had possessed for Mme Carpentier
and when she asked them what their ages were Hedwig
said she was thirty-one, Ilsa said she was seventy-three
and Hannah said she was a hundred and forty-four. After
that Mme Carpentier said they were the worst-behaved
girls she had ever had the misfortune to teach and made
them conjugate irregular verbs for the remaining forty-five
minutes.

The other thing was that Mutti seemed to have changed
her opinion of Mr Tozer. Although she continued to nod
to him when they met by chance in the lounge, there was
a coldness about her manner. She was heard to say that
she had been mistaken about Mr Tozer, that he was not as
gentlemanly as he first appeared and that M. Delavacquerie
had hinted that he was erratic in settling his bills. And
Hannah thought that this was hard on Mr Tozer, who
seemed to spend his time sitting meekly in the lounge,
walking on the esplanade or occasionally going into Toulon
on the bus, and appeared to live an entirely blameless existence. When she considered this at length, she decided it
was further evidence of Mutti being a poor fish. Over the
next week she noted other instances of this fundamental
weakness. There was the way Mutti glanced suspiciously
around the restaurant as they made their way into it, as if
she feared contamination at the hands of whoever lurked
within it. There was the haughty manner in which she
addressed M. Delavacquerie and Albert. And there was
the way she detached stamps that the postal authorities had
omitted to frank from their envelopes and put them away
in the drawer of her escritoire in the bedroom for further

use. Hannah realised that she had reached a stage in her life when she had to be dispassionate about her mother, and this awareness both exhilarated her and depressed her. On the one hand, she was pleased to have acquired an air of detachment, which seemed to her an important thing to possess, whereas on the other she suspected that, when applied to such a person as Mutti, this objectivity could only lead to trouble.

It was November now, and the weather was sometimes too bad to go out in the afternoon. Despite these obstacles, Hannah paid several more visits to the hut, and on one occasion managed to smuggle out a small tray hidden in the folds of her mackintosh. She was pleased with the hut and its current state and felt thoroughly at home there, but at the same time determined that nobody else – or rather, no one not of her choosing – should find out about it. In the second week of November it was her birthday, and they celebrated by having a tea-party in the lounge at which Mutti presented her with an ivory hair-slide and Ilsa and Hedwig produced a scarf that they had managed to knit in the evenings without her noticing. Mr Tozer, who had not been invited to the party but happened to be in the room at the time, congratulated her and said that fifteen was a very serious age. When the party was over and they had eaten the slices of cake that M. Delavacquerie had brought to the table, Mutti said unexpectedly that despite all the activities that had been arranged for them she felt they were getting into a rut. Consequently, she suggested that on the following day they should get the bus into Toulon and spend the day enjoying themselves. And though the girls could not exactly see how they were supposed to enjoy themselves in Toulon they nodded their heads and agreed that it was a good idea.

The day in Toulon was not entirely a success. To begin with the bus that plied the coast road broke down and they had to wait at the roadside in the cold for nearly half-an-hour until a second vehicle came to rescue them. Then it turned out that there was not a great deal to do in Toulon, where most of the shops seemed to be closed and it was, additionally, raining quite hard. In the end, when they had inspected the old fort and looked at the handful of soldiers who were in attendance, they went and sat in a café and ate some buns and looked at the rain and some picturesque fishermen who were attempting to mend their nets. And Mutti said that there would come a time when they should not have to live in a hotel in Sanary-sur-Mer and soon things would look up. There was only one minor excitement. This came on the return journey when they discovered, to their surprise, that Mr Tozer was sitting at the back of the bus. He had had his hair cut and smiled several times to himself in a way that, Hannah thought, could not possibly have been provoked by the book he was reading, which was called *Berlin Alexanderplatz*.

By this time the hut, in addition to the carpet, the foot-stool, the teacups and the tray, had acquired a picture of Herr von Ribbentrop cut out of a newspaper. Seeing these ornaments spread out before her, Hannah thought that the moment had come for a decisive step. Accordingly, the next time they happened to be alone together in the lounge, she went across to Mr Tozer as he sat reading and said: 'I would be very honoured if you would take tea with me this afternoon.' Initially Mr Tozer was nonplussed, but appreciated the seriousness of what was afoot. He put down *Berlin Alexanderplatz,* crossed one of his legs over the other, and said: 'Do you mean that we should have tea together here in the hotel?' And Hannah explained about the hut on the edge of the dunes and the efforts she had made to spruce it up, whereupon Mr Tozer nodded, as if he had been expecting something of the sort, got up from his chair – he had very long legs, like a grasshopper's, and said that he would be delighted to accept her invitation, and would her sisters be present? When Hannah said they would not, he nodded again and said he perfectly understood.

There were several difficulties about that afternoon, although some of them only became apparent in retrospect. The first was the rain, which fell in torrents, stopped abruptly and then fell intermittently for several hours. The second was Mutti and the girls, who seemed to think that she would want to construct card-castles with them on a green baize table in the lounge and were disappointed when she refused. The third was providing anything for Mr Tozer and herself to drink. In the end she remembered the existence of a thermos flask that was kept in one of the trunks in Mutti's bedroom took it into the kitchen and filled it with a quantity of black coffee that she brewed up on the stove. This, she thought, would be sufficient for Mr Tozer, who in any case would probably be more interested in talking about the book he was reading and the poems he was writing than in what he was offered to drink. The rain beat upon the window while she was brewing the coffee and she heard the smash of a roof-tile dislodged by the wind onto the concrete. That lunchtime they had *loups de mer* again, which everybody agreed were quite disgusting.

It was about half-past two when she finally managed to get away and the afternoon was already turning grey. There was more rain scudding in horizontally from the west and the sky was a gunmetal colour. Mr Tozer was already waiting outside the hut when she arrived. He was wearing an Aquascutum raincoat and a trilby hat and looked so like one of the Englishmen you saw in films that it was a shame nobody had told him. When she came up to where he stood she said: 'It is very nice of you to have come,' but she did not say 'How was your journey?', which was what her mother always said to people at parties, on the grounds that she knew very well Mr Tozer had only walked from the hotel. There was an awkwardness about this, but it was relieved by Mr Tozer's good nature. Once inside the hut he spent several minutes admiring the arrangements and dealt with the drawback of there only being a footstool by squatting on his haunches. Neither was he put out by there only being black coffee.

'Actually,' he said, 'at fashionable tea-parties black coffee is really the only thing that anyone drinks.'

She was so glad to hear about this that she said: had he written any more poems recently? But Mr Tozer said that poetry was not like writing an essay or a piece of journalism for a newspaper, that you could not force it and it had to evolve on its own terms.

'Could I have a cigarette?' she said. 'I'm dying for a cigarette.' She had only smoked a cigarette twice in her life before, but she was confident that she could disguise this fact. Mr Tozer offered her a cigarette from a silver case with the initials H.R. de T. engraved on it, and took one himself, and she smoked hers in little nervous puffs, screwing up her eyes when the smoke got into them and tapping the ash at intervals onto the sand. While she was doing this she looked at Mr Tozer and decided that he was not as nice-looking as she had first thought, that his chin was too weak and that, though tall, there was something spindly about him. But she liked his hair and his small, neatly pruned moustache.

'Shall you be going back to London soon?' she asked.

'Oh I don't live in London,' Mr Tozer said. 'If I go anywhere, it will be to Paris. But, you see, I like it here. I like walking along the beach. I like getting on with my work. And I like the *ambience*.'

She wondered what he meant by this. Outside she could hear the tumult of the rain falling on the roof. Sometimes some of the drops were louder than the others. Then after a while they became quite unindividuated again. She noticed that the photograph of Herr von Ribbentrop she had cut out of the newspaper was beginning to turn yellow at the edges and that Mr Tozer had begun to breathe rather heavily. A bit later he leaned forward and put his hand on her knee. But this she thought she could deal with. She tapped Mr Tozer's exploring forefinger with the edge of her willow-pattern teacup and he – rather shamefacedly, she thought – withdrew it. She did not especially want Mr Tozer to put his hand on her knee, she decided, but the manner of his withdrawing it made her think that, like her mother, he was a poor fish. When Mr Tozer had got his breath back he said: 'I was glad your mother had a good time in Munich,' and she replied: 'I must be getting back. Mutti will be wondering where I am.' Outside the rain continued to fall.

◊

Two days after this M. Delavacquerie put up a notice on
the green-baize board in the vestibule where letters that
arrived for people who had long ago left the hotel were
displayed which said that the hotel would be absolutely
closed for the two weeks either side of Christmas. Mutti
was extremely put out by this information, claiming that
it contradicted previous advice that she had been given
and that it confirmed her low opinion of M. Delvacquerie
who did not, when it came to it, know how to run a hotel.
'But where shall we go now?' Hedwig asked, and Mutti
said that if the matter proved insoluble they would rent a
house in the village for the duration, or possibly go to their
relatives in Wurttemberg.

Meanwhile, the girls continued to keep up their scrapbook. They stuck in a story from the local newspaper about
a porpoise that had been washed up on the beach, a leaf
from one of the plane trees on the esplanade and one of
the bus tickets from the trip to Toulon. All this, Mutti
said, would give their father an excellent idea of how they
had spent their time in Sanary-sur-Mer, and that he would
appreciate its thoroughness, and Hannah, who had never
known their father to appreciate that quality, wondered if
she was right about this. Mr Tozer continued to haunt the
lounge and did not seem to be in the least embarrassed by
what had happened, or had not happened, in the hut. In
which connection, Hannah found that she was visiting
the hut less often. There were several reasons for this. The
first was that the weather was so bad, especially in the
afternoons, as to render walking on the beach inadvisable.

The second was that the hut was irrevocably associated in her mind with Mr Tozer's long, lean, hair-beknuckled hand receding like a spider across the space between them. The third was a feeling that she had simply exhausted its possibilities, had reached a stage in its redecoration and refurbishment on which it would be difficult to build without resources which she did not possess. In some ways this was oddly satisfying. She had done all she could do, she thought, and derived pleasure from the doing. But now it was time to be moving on.

In the first week of December Mutti announced that she had decided how they would spend the Christmas period. The girls listened with interest, but in the end what Mutti had to say was unexciting. She explained that despite her entreaties M. Delavaquerie would not agree to keep the hotel open for the festive season, as he and his family wanted to spend it with Mme Delavacquerie's aunt in Brittany. Given these unfortunate circumstances, they would spend Christmas with their relatives in Wurttemberg, and the week after it staying in a fisherman's cottage which was available to rent. That afternoon they went to inspect the fisherman's cottage, which was unexpectedly spacious but smelled of salt and was heated only by an oil stove, but Mutti said they would enjoy roughing it for the few days they were obliged to spend there and that their father would be interested to hear of their adventures. On the way back to the hotel, while Ilsa and Hedwig played a game that involved tipping the brim of each other's berets and shrieking with laughter, Hannah, who was cross about the Christmas arrangements and determined to cause mischief, said:

'Mutti, tell me, why do you so much dislike Mr Tozer?'

Mutti's face, she saw, wore the same expression as when she had seen M. Delavacquerie's notice on the green-baize board.

'I do not dislike Mr Tozer. In fact, nothing could be further from the case. What makes you think that I do?'

'You never seem to wish to talk to him as much as you did. He looks lonely. Surely it would be nice for him to have someone to talk to?'

'Mr Tozer is one of those people one sees in hotels. There is no reason to talk to him. None. And why should you think Mr Tozer lonely? I know he receives many letters. And I believe he has friends in Toulon that he goes to visit.'

Hannah wondered how Mutti knew about the friends Mr Tozer apparently had in Toulon, but decided not to press the matter. The person who owned the fisherman's cottage turned out to be not, as was previously supposed, a fisherman but a notary who had an office in Marseille. This was very inconvenient, as Mutti was compelled to take a taxi all the way there to negotiate with him. On the day that she did this the wind lifted and it stopped raining, so Hannah put on her mackintosh and went along the beach to the hut. It was a week or more since she had last visited and the interior was showing signs of neglect. The picture postcard of Claudette Colbert had nearly disintegrated, the mirror was even more speckled with rust and a rip had developed in one of the sheets of tar paper. The two willow pattern cups she had taken from the kitchen were still lying on the square of carpet, and for some reason she could not explain she picked them up and hurled them against the wall, where they shattered into several pieces. The ends of the two cigarettes she and Mr Tozer had smoked were not far away and she ground them into fragments with her heel. Afterwards she went and inspected the grey, choppy sea and thought about what lay beyond it: Berber tribesmen leading their camels to palm-fringed wadis; giant hibiscuses gleaming in the sun; fires burning in the mountains. She suspected that in reality Africa was not in the least like that, but this was the way she preferred to conceive it.

That night, not long after they had gone to bed, Hedwig woke up with one of her stomach aches. In ordinary circumstances Hannah would have let her lie, but this stomach ache seemed to be particularly bad. In fact, there was a distinct possibility that Hedwig was going to be sick. Bored by Hedwig's infirmities, Hannah decided that Mutti could deal with this. Accordingly, she put on her dressing-gown, told Ilsa that if Hedwig really was ill she should fetch the jug from the side table and encourage her to be sick into that, and went out into the corridor. Here it was pitch dark and she could hear the wind rushing against the roof, together with a noise of whispering voices. These seemed to be coming from her mother's room. To her surprise, when she knocked on the door, it was opened by Mr Tozer. He, too, was wearing a dressing-gown and his spectacles were pushed down to the front of his nose.

'What may I do for you Hannah?' He did not seem abashed that he should be found in Mutti's room in his dressing-gown. Although the door was open only a few inches and there was not very much light, she could see her mother's figure in the corner of the room next to the wardrobe.

'It's Hedwig,' she explained. 'She is not feeling at all

well. We thought that Mutti ought to come and see her.'

'You had better tell her I shall be with her shortly,' Mutti said.

'That's right,' Mr Tozer added. He was standing rather awkwardly on the balls of his feet as if he was about to spring up into the air. 'Tell your sister that her mother will be with her in a moment. Tell her to keep her spirits up.'

There was clearly nothing more to be said. Hannah went back to their room to find that Hedwig had not been able to contain herself, nor Ilsa get to the jug in time, so that there was sick all over the bedsheets. She was about to tell the girls what she had seen in Mutti's room, but in the end she decided to forgo this pleasure on the grounds that people, herself included, were entitled to their secrets.

Mr Tozer left by taxi on the following afternoon. He did not say goodbye. In his absence a kind of torpor descended on the hotel. Hedwig, who had been sick several more times during the night, went back to their room to sleep. Even though the weather was not at all good, Mutti went out onto the terrace with a sheaf of notepaper and sat writing letters. After a while she abandoned the letter-writing and stared out to sea at the grey sky and the boiling waves. And Hannah, looking at her every so often through the window of the lounge, thought that she sympathised with her mother, but not infinitely so. Her own life, she thought, was not going to be like this. She could not imagine how it could be made to differ from the existence she currently led, but she was confident that in certain crucial respects it was in her power to effect this transformation and that, in the fullness of time, she would find herself sitting around a table at Gstaad with Herr von Ribbentrop and people whose names appeared in the *Almanach de Gotha*, while crisp white sunshine fell on snow-capped crags, and she smiled and drank glasses of hock, and looked with satisfaction at the slopes above her, full of sleek, sinuous figures making their patterns, endlessly crossing and recrossing in bright Alpine air.

Acknowledgements

I SHOULD LIKE to acknowledge the influence of Annie Proulx on 'Moving On.' Many thanks to Chris and Jen at Salt, and to my agent Gordon Wise. Much love, as ever, to Rachel, Felix, Benjy and Leo.

This book has been typeset by
SALT PUBLISHING LIMITED
using Granjon, a font designed by George W. Jones
for the British branch of the Linotype
company in the United Kingdom. It has been
manufactured using Holmen Book Cream
65gsm paper, and printed and bound by Clays
Limited in Bungay, Suffolk, Great Britain.

CROMER
GREAT BRITAIN
MMXXV